A Kiss at Midsummer

Copyright © 2019 by Meg Easton

Cover Illustration: Once Upon a Cover

Interior design: Mountain Heights Publishing

Author website: www.megeaston.com

Also by Meg Easton

Romancing the Spy romantic comedies

Spies Don't Fall for Their Asset

Spies Don't Fall for Their Rival

Spiced Chais and Secret Spies

Holiday Lights and Cocoa Cookie Nights

Spies Don't Fall for Their Neighbor (coming 2025)

~

How to Not Fall romantic comedies

How to Not Fall for the Guy Next Door

How to Not Fall for the Wrong Guy

How to Not Fall for Your Best Friend

How to Not Fall for Your Ex

~

Nestled Hollow Romances

Coming Home to the Top of Main Street

Second Chance on the Corner of Main Street

Christmas at the End of Main Street

More than Friends in the Middle of Main Street

Love Again at the Heart of Main Street

More than Enemies on the Bridge of Main Street

❧

<h2 style="text-align:center">A Mountain Springs Christmas</h2>

The Christmas Pact

The Christmas Bet

The Christmas Clause

❧

<h2 style="text-align:center">Love Started Romances</h2>

It Started with a Sunset

It Started with a Note

It Started with a Glance

❧

<h2 style="text-align:center">Silver Leaf Falls romance</h2>

Coming Home to Silver Leaf Falls

A Kiss at Midsummer

A Kiss at Midsummer

MEG EASTON

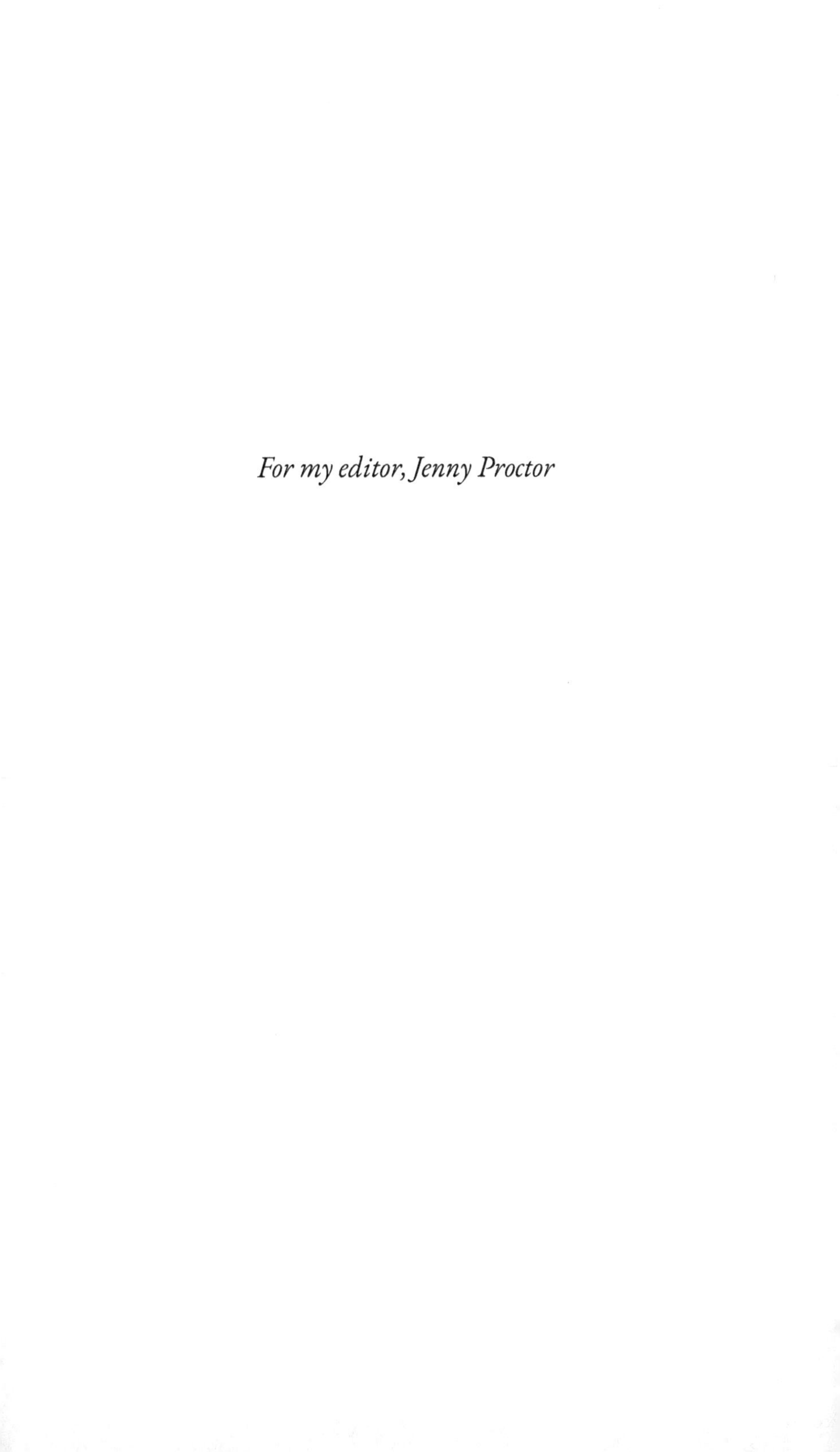

For my editor, Jenny Proctor

Contents

A Kiss at Midsummer

One

MERIT

Perfect business days like today always made Merit Casselman swirl with two very different emotions: elation and fear. Elation that a business he and Graham started from nothing not long ago had made it big enough to be on the cover of Business Success magazine. And fear that the success was too good to be true and would come crashing down on them at any instant. It always made him feel like he had to hold tightly to the business so the business would know how much he didn't want it to slip away.

The energy in their meeting had been incredible. Merit thanked his executive staff—all of whom were older than both he and Graham—for coming to their weekly meeting and for working so hard to get them to where they were. As they all left the conference room chatting about exciting new ideas, Merit's business partner, Graham, leaned back in his chair, looking out the floor-to-ceiling windows that spanned the west wall.

Merit had too much to do to kick back like Graham did, though. He scooted next to Carla, his motherly personal assistant who seemed to be able to stay on top of everything at once and made sure that she had put on his calendar when to check back with each executive about every action item.

Then he stood, notepad in hand, and looked at the screen that filled the wall at the head of the table. All the pertinent numbers for each section of the company were displayed in easy-to-read graphs in front of him. He looked between the images and his notes about all the ideas for their company that had come to him during the meeting, deciding which they should pursue first.

Without taking his eyes off the information in front of him, he said over his shoulder, "Carla, what's my next meeting?"

"It's in two minutes, and it's with Graham."

Merit turned around, his eyebrows creasing together. "Graham, we have a meeting? I don't remember seeing it on my schedule this morning."

Graham just smiled, still leaning back in his chair, his hands locked behind his head like he was sunbathing on the beach.

Carla said, "It's on the schedule—he's your two o'clock."

"Huh."

Carla gathered up her things and then left the conference room, closing the door behind her.

Graham stood and joined Merit in looking at the screen. "It's a pretty cool feeling, isn't it? None of that money in those charts would be possible if it weren't for our company making the software you're using to look at it."

Merit smiled. They had known they had a pretty special idea back when they were a twenty-two-year-old Computer Science major and a twenty-year-old business major having their first brainstorming sessions in college. "Who would've guessed that we'd become this successful in just six years?"

"We've done some incredible things," Graham said, holding the remote out and clicking the screen off.

Merit had assumed that this unexpected meeting was going to be about the information on the screen, so, curious, he followed Graham to the side of the long table and leaned against it next to him, looking out over their company's half a dozen buildings and the mountains beyond.

"Do you remember college?"

"Yeah," Merit said, surprised at the abrupt change in topic. "Best two years of my life."

"We had some pretty great times. You, me, Noah, Saint, Ian. Chumming around, making mischief, playing games, having fun."

Merit nodded. Some great times indeed. His phone was in his pocket, with the ZentCube app installed on it. He hadn't quite gotten enough time to look at today's numbers, and he was itching to pull it out and check everything.

"What did you like best?"

Merit laughed. "All of it. It was the first time—well since I was eleven—that I only had to worry about myself. I could just focus on soaking in all the learning, and choosing how I was going to spend any free time."

"Do you remember how much fun we had, brainstorming ZentCube for hours?"

"We were young and didn't know enough about the world yet to know how impossible all our dreams were."

"It wasn't, though—we pulled it off. And we're still young. Except somewhere along the way, we stopped having fun doing it."

The comment surprised Merit, especially coming from Graham. The guy constantly looked relaxed, chill, and happy. He somehow managed to still get out and have fun, have hobbies, go on adventures, vacation—all of it, regardless of how much there was to do. He even did it consistently enough to find himself a wife. Merit had no idea how he found the time to do any of it. "Are you trying to say you aren't having fun anymore?"

From the corner of his eye, Merit could see his friend lift a shoulder in a shrug. "It's fun. It's not the only fun out there, and sometimes I just really want to grab hold of the next adventure. But what I'm concerned about is that *you* aren't having fun anymore."

"I'm having fun," Merit said, his defenses rising. "Running a business as successful as ours is fun." So much fun, in fact, that it was all Merit wanted to do. His notebook was sitting on the table behind him, and he wanted to have some fun right now looking over his ideas and thinking about which ones he wanted to move on.

"There's more to life than this business. And the irony of it is, the more you get out and live a life outside the business, the better the business will do. When you open yourself up to new experiences, you expand your creativity. You'll lead this company better if you step away from it every day. If you're willing to boot it out and give the head space to other things."

Merit shook his head, his arms folded, looking out at the clouds hiding the sun, casting shadows on his mountains. "We've got a lot of people depending on us to run this right. That takes one hundred percent focus." Graham wasn't going to convince him otherwise, so he might as well stop trying.

"These last two years have been good for me," Graham said. "It's amazing how much more," he paused, seeming to try to find the right words, "*complete* I am with a wife. She brings me more clarity, balance, and focus than I've ever had before. I want that for you, too."

Merit actually laughed. "Just because you found a soulmate and are blissfully married doesn't mean you have to push it on everyone else. A wife wouldn't bring me all those things—she would just be a distraction. I wouldn't have time for her, so I'd just feel guilty about never having time for her."

"Only because you spend one hundred percent of your time here. There's more to life than that."

Merit didn't agree. He had zero interest in pursuing anything other than this business's security and growth.

In a quieter voice, Graham said, "I think your mom would agree, too."

Merit's eyes flashed to Graham and then narrowed. He knew better than to use his mom to try to convince him.

Graham let out a slow, defeated breath. Then he turned to face Merit, but Merit didn't mirror the move; he just kept looking straight ahead. "Here's the thing, Merit. The baby's going to be here in five months, and Tessa and I want to move to the suburbs and get ourselves the smiling neighbors bringing by cookies, the dog, the white picket fence, the whole nine yards. And," he nodded his head at the scene out of the window, "I want to send a few business ideas I've got out there, and see how they do."

None of that sounded appealing to Merit, and he could feel his whole body revolting at even the idea of it.

"But I can't do any of that if I'm tied up here daily."

Merit shifted Graham's direction, his heart racing, confusion, disbelief, and surprise all competing for dominance. "What are you saying, Graham?"

"I'm saying that I want to make you a deal. I know you've wanted fifty-one percent ownership since the beginning. I might be willing to sell you two percent, but only under certain conditions."

Merit stood taller and dropped his arms, turning fully toward Graham. *No way.* He had been dreaming about this for so long, he didn't even dare let himself hope that Graham was serious.

Back when they'd first started the business, Graham was graduating from college, and as the one two years older and from a family that wasn't as destitute as Merit's, he was able to put more into their fledgling business. They had agreed that Graham would own fifty-one percent of the company and Merit would own forty-nine.

Back then, it had been the difference of a few hundred dollars. Now it was the difference of several million dollars. For the past five years, Merit had been trying to talk Graham into selling him the two percent, making Merit the controlling shareholder, but Graham hadn't ever been even close to budging.

"What are the conditions?" Merit was sure he would do pretty much anything. Pay anything. Sacrifice anything.

"You go on vacation."

Merit cocked his head to the side, sure he didn't hear correctly.

"Or more specifically," Graham said, walking back around to the other side of the table, pulling a portfolio out of his bag, and sliding it across the table to Merit, "going on a vacation that I plan."

Merit picked up the case and flipped through it, seeing lots of papers—some typed, some brochures, some itineraries, but not taking in any of it. Too many other thoughts were running through his head to comprehend anything in his hands.

"You need to figure out how to have fun again, and how to think about things other than this company. Because I'm not going to walk away and give you controlling interest in a company that we've poured so much into if you can't refuel yourself creatively."

"And you think that me going on vacation is going to do that? Sold." Merit slapped the portfolio down on the table top.

"No, I don't. That's why I have more stipulations."

Graham walked around the table, opened the case, and pulled out a full-sized, full-color booklet that had to be a good twenty pages. The front cover said *The Royal Palm at Myrtle Beach, South Carolina* in metallic gold lettering.

Graham opened it to the center of the brochure, where across both pages it showed the kind of resort they had dreamed about back when they had been stupid college kids with a business idea.

Merit narrowed his eyes, suddenly distrusting everything this portfolio contained. "What stipulations?"

Graham cleared his throat and held up a finger. "You go to this resort. They've got some mansions right on the beach, complete with private beach access. I've rented you a modest-sized one for four weeks. You have to stay there every night during those four weeks."

"Four weeks?" Merit practically shouted. "How am I supposed to run this business from the other side of the country for *four weeks*?"

"Two," Graham said, holding up a second finger, "you refrain from running this business for those four weeks."

Merit looked at Graham, dumbfounded. This business didn't just run itself.

"I know this business is in your thoughts twenty-four-seven, and the only way you're going to get away from that is if you go cold turkey. So during those four weeks, you won't have access to the ZentCube app, so no company data. No email. No phone calls for information. No getting company information in any way."

Merit broke out in a cold sweat. All they had worked for

could vanish in four weeks, and he would return to a company on the verge of bankruptcy.

Graham rolled his eyes. "Stop with the doomsday expressions. *You* are not the only thing keeping this company running. I don't know if you've noticed how capable your business partner is at all of it," Graham said, gesturing at himself. "And our executive team has some of the best leaders in the nation. We've got this. I give you my word that you'll come back to see that this company is just as shiny as when you left it. Your company email account will auto-forward to me, so you don't need to worry that an important ball will get dropped."

He couldn't do this! Whenever he flew anywhere on a business trip, he got in-flight wifi because he couldn't go an hour without any information on his company. It was an impossible thing to ask. Simply impossible. He was so light-headed that he couldn't stay standing, so he pulled out a chair and collapsed into it.

But he couldn't pass up an offer to buy Graham's two percent. He had waited so many years for this and the opportunity might not ever come along again.

"Graham, I get what you're saying, buddy. You need me to do things outside of work. I will join a biking team, a painting class, a movie club, a roller derby team—you name it. Anything that will get me doing something other than this business every week. We don't need to do something this drastic. What would this even accomplish?"

"I would explain it, but you wouldn't believe me if I did. You're just going to have to trust me that by the time the four weeks are up, you'll understand exactly what it accomplished. Now quiet—I'm not done." He held up a third finger. "Three: I have hired the activities director at the resort to be your personal activities director. She has been instructed to give you different experiences every single day. They're not negotiable."

Merit opened his mouth, but before he could say anything, Graham held up finger number four.

"And last but not least, let's talk about departure. Your plane leaves at five."

Merit's eyes flew open and he stood up so quickly that the chair rolled several feet behind him. "What? Today?!"

Graham grinned and slid the portfolio to him. "Your itinerary is in here. So's the list of the four requirements, just in case you got stuck on number two and stopped listening. I sent Carla to your house this morning to pack everything you will need for the full four weeks. Your luggage is downstairs in your driver's trunk, and he's ready to drive you to the airport anytime in the next hour."

"I have a three o'clock appointment. And a three-thirty. And a five. And tomorrow..."

"Nope. Your entire schedule has been cleared. There's nothing for you to do here for the next four weeks."

"Why? Why so soon? Give me a few weeks to get everything prepared for a four-week absence." It was suddenly too hot in this room. Way too hot. He loosened his tie and unbuttoned his top button. His legs felt weak, but he couldn't sit, so he leaned into both hands on the table.

"That would defeat the purpose. And besides, my baby

isn't getting any younger. Now, are you in? If you're willing to do this, every single bit of it, I'll have the paperwork ready and waiting for your signature to switch two percent over to you, giving you controlling interest in the company when you get back. What do you say?"

Merit let out a long slow breath and closed his eyes for several moments. He had done hard things all through his life. He did hard things every single day. He could do this. In the end, it would all be worth it. It would be worth it. He could endure anything for four weeks if it meant two percent at the end.

He swallowed hard, then opened his eyes and said, "Okay. We have a deal."

Two

ELISE

ELISE STEVENS WALKED into her apartment after her late meeting with her boss, Cyree Hue. Graham McNeil, some wealthy business owner in Denver, had been working with Cyree for the past couple of weeks to see if he could get a personal Activities Director for his business partner.

And since "every guest at The Royal Palm is royalty and should be treated as such," they had been working to rearrange her schedule so she could accommodate the man, and everything had finally worked out.

Right before she had left the meeting with Cyree, though, her boss had said, "I know you understand the rules, but I'm going to say it anyway. This is a VIP client, and you're going to be spending a lot of time with him. You're expected to behave professionally at all times—no flirting, no dating, even if he ends up being young and attractive."

"Come on, Cyree," Elise had said. "You know that my loyalty to the resort always comes first."

The truth was, she was a little hurt that Cyree would've even brought it up—Elise had never given her any reason to. But then Cyree gave her a warm smile that told Elise that she was trusted. "And that's exactly why we okayed this arrangement."

Cyree had let the man know that Elise was going to be available, and let Elise know to expect a video chat from Graham to work out the details. What she hadn't expected when she answered the video call was, well, all the details. Now that she and Graham were chatting, he was giving so many details.

"Cyree and I have already worked out the details of payment to the resort," Graham said. "That will cover the hours you'll be spending with Merit. But now I need to ask, as the activities director, do you often get tips?"

"I do." A spark of hope made her breathe a little easier. Tips weren't a huge chunk of her paycheck, but she had set goals for saving money, and not being able to earn the tips she normally would while working with this man's business partner was going to compromise those goals. Maybe the man was going to offer to tip her what she normally would be making.

"Good, good. I'm glad The Royal Palm doesn't frown on that, because I have a proposition for you."

Elise nodded for him to continue.

"Look, my business partner, Merit, needs to learn how to date and have fun again. To remember how to connect with humans outside of work. I think going on a few dates would be good for the guy, but his flirting skills are a tad rusty. I don't want you to set him up on dates. Just be his wingman and help him find a few dates—let's say five—and just give him a nudge, maybe a few tips. I've got a big fat bonus at the end of this for you."

"I can't say I've ever accepted a tip for being a wingman before."

Graham chuckled. "Wingwoman, then. But listen, I want the dates to be guests who he seems to actually be interested in. I want him to remember what it's like to be attracted to something other than work."

The more Graham talked about this man, the more Elise realized how difficult the task might be.

"Help him find those five dates, and I know he'll be able to meet the requirements I've set for him. If he does, the bonus is yours."

Elise nodded. "I'll do everything I can. You can work out the details of the bonus with Cyree."

"I..." the man hesitated, "would rather not."

She cocked her head to the side.

"Listen. Merit isn't just my business partner—he's also been my best friend for the past eight years. I just want the guy to be happy, and he's got a better chance at being that way if he figures out that there's a whole rich life waiting for him outside of work. I don't mind that people know I've hired you as his activity director. But as far as the dating aspect—well, I'm not looking to embarrass him, so the fewer people who know the more sensitive details, the better."

Elise nodded. If the roles were reversed and a friend of

Elise's sent her on some kind of intervention vacation and the friend asked a guy to help her figure out how to date, she would definitely appreciate fewer people knowing. "I understand, and I will use discretion."

"Good," Graham said, leaning back in his chair, smiling from ear to ear. "Does twenty thousand sound okay for the bonus?"

Elise nearly choked. *Twenty thousand?* That was easily ten times the amount she could possibly earn in tips during that four weeks. She wanted to question the number out loud, just to make sure she heard correctly, but there was no way to do that and still seem professional. So she just nodded and said, "That would be great," in her most businesslike voice.

When they ended the call, she stood up from the chair at her kitchen table and whistled her way to the freezer. She glanced at the closed door down the hall that was empty in the off-season but now housed her summer season roommate and co-worker, HallieMae. She wanted to tell her friend about the video call, but she was currently on a date with the guy she was crushing on who worked at the Mini Palm. Elise didn't mind waiting until tomorrow morning to chat, though. Tonight was just her and that was perfect.

She pulled a pint of Chunky Monkey out of the freezer then grabbed a spoon and headed into her bedroom. She knew that Graham wouldn't have offered a massive bonus if he had expected her job to be easy. She knew to be wary of this guy, Merit Casselman, who was supposed to arrive sometime later tonight and would be showing up at their first meeting tomorrow at nine, but she wasn't going to think about that tonight. Tonight she was going to bask in her good fortune.

She put the ice cream and spoon on her nightstand, then walked over to the bulletin board that hung on the wall straight out from the foot of her bed. There were exactly four things pinned to the board: a picture of the home she'd spent her entire childhood living in; the phone number of the couple who owned it and who had recently let her know that they wanted to sell it; the loan papers that showed exactly how much money she would need to have in the bank if she wanted to make an offer on the house; and a cheesy graph she had made showing the total amount needed, complete with a red square filled in for each one hundred dollars she had saved toward that goal.

Picking up the red marker she used to fill in the squares, she drew a line right at the top of the graph. If she managed to get this businessman who only cared about his business and making money to do all of the requirements that Graham laid out, the twenty thousand dollar bonus that Graham was offering would put her over the top on her chart.

Elise flopped onto her bed, picked up the celebratory ice cream and spoon, and savored every spoonful of nutty, banana-y, chocolatey goodness as she gazed at her bulletin board, joy at what could potentially be hers in four short weeks filling her to the top.

Elise's toes sunk into the sand as she set the volleyball in an arc toward her partner, HallieMae, who spiked it over the net. Another one of her employees, Kale, dove for the ball and missed.

"How are the kids' activities looking this week, Zabrena?"

Zabrena tossed the ball over the net to her. "Good. I've got a scavenger hunt through the resort lined up for this morning and painting this afternoon. Both are full. Most of the activities this week are full, actually."

"Five to three," she said, serving the ball. "Good. Do you need help with anything?"

Zabrena hit the volleyball back over the net, nice and easy right to HallieMae. "I probably will for the macaroni art project on Friday afternoon."

HallieMae sent it back to their side not-so-nice-and-easy.

"I can help," Kale said, hitting the ball back to them, then motioning at the ball as it came Elise's direction. "Obviously I helped with that beautiful shot, but I meant on Friday."

Elise set herself right under the ball, clasping her hands together, arms straight. "And how about the teens, HallieMae?"

During college, Elise hadn't had a home to go to during the summers, so she took classes during the summer semesters, too, in order to keep her student housing. It meant she graduated a week before her twenty-first birthday, and spent that first summer at The Royal Palm on the activities committee—in the same job position that HallieMae was now working. By the end of that summer, Cyree had been so impressed with her that she offered her the job of Activities Director, and she'd been doing it now for three years.

Her favorite thing about being a manager and having her own staff was the freedom to have their team meetings on one of the beach volleyball courts by the staff cottages. The court was on permanent reserve on Wednesday mornings at eight for them, and it quickly became one of her favorite times of the week. It was way better than leading some dull meeting in some stuffy conference room.

HallieMae updated her on the activities planned for the teens as they played, then Kale talked about the special events they had coming up over the next month as they played in the sand, the slight breeze bringing along with it the salty scent of the waves, the sun rising over the ocean and spilling its warmth and goodness down on them.

"And," Kale said, jumping high next to the net, spiking the ball, "the plans for the Midsummer Ball are coming along nicely."

Elise dove for the ball he spiked and managed to hit it, but it only went a couple of feet in the air and HallieMae couldn't get under it enough to hit it back over the net. HallieMae tossed the ball to Zabrena.

"So," Kale said as he watched the ball arc over the net. "I heard you're going to be a private activities director for some super-rich guy."

Elise flashed a look at HallieMae. Her staff member

motioned at herself and shook her head in an *It wasn't me who spilled the beans* way.

She shook her head. "I am." It probably shouldn't surprise her that her staff already knew—they were a tight-knit group. Still, though, it had barely been an hour since she had told HallieMae, and Cyree was the only other person who knew. Not that she hadn't planned on telling them at this meeting anyway.

"I video-chatted with the man's business partner last night. He's hoping I can get the guy to relax if I take him on enough excursions and events, and from what he wants, it sounds like it's going to keep me extra busy over the next four weeks. Do you three mind stepping in when I get too tied up to cover all the things I normally do?"

They all grinned and nodded like trained dolphins. HallieMae was her only full-time employee, and the others were always eager to get more hours. That, and they all really liked to play and have fun and by helping her out as needed, they got paid for it.

"I heard he's a middle-aged curmudgeon," Zabrena said. "Is it true?"

Elise's eyes cut to HallieMae, and this time she gave a sheepish *Okay, I'll admit it was me—I just couldn't help it* shrug.

"Why?" Elise asked. "Are you looking to set him up with your mom?"

Zabrena lifted a shoulder. "He's middle-aged, single, and rich." She ticked each item off on her fingers. "So he would pretty much solve all of her problems."

"You can't set him up with your mom," Elise said, pulling out her *because I'm the boss and I said so voice*, even though it even made her cringe. "And just a reminder that you all signed non-disclosure agreements, so no letting anyone outside of Royal Palm staff know who is a guest here. The rule even applies when it's a man whose name you've never even heard before."

"So I can't tell my mom his name," Zabrena said as they all walked to a nearby table to grab drinks from their water bottles, "and I can't set him up with my mom. But what I'm hearing is that I *can* invite my mom to come see me some afternoon when I'm running an event near where you're going to be, right?"

Elise chuckled. "Zabrena, you're killing me! I'm pretty sure that the 'staff can't date guests' rule applies to setting up our family members, too. Besides, your mom deserves someone way better than some rich dude who can only think about his money and his business and doesn't remember how to have fun."

She glanced down at her watch, then let out a strained yelp. "Our first meeting is in ten minutes!" She looked down at her fitted t-shirt and shorts and started brushing off the sand that seemed to cover every inch of them. "I wasn't going to play hard today so I wouldn't get all sweaty and gross."

"Yeah, like that would ever happen," Kale said. "Do you want us to pour our water bottles on your arms and legs to rinse you off?"

Elise pondered it for half a second, then slung her bag

over her head and shoved in her water bottle. "No. I've got to stop by the activities rooms to get my things. I'll just run there and take a few moments to clean up before heading to the clubhouse." She started jogging off, and called out, "Find me if you need me," then she switched into an all-out run.

She ran up the palm tree and shrub-lined path and onto the sidewalks, racing past perfectly manicured lawns, stone statues, flower beds, and benches. She rounded one of the pools—the one that attracted families with small kids—and slowed down as she came to a group of elderly couples out for a morning walk, chatting and laughing and not noticing that they were taking up all the space and going at a speed that was too impossible to walk at when she was this far behind schedule.

She found an opening and jogged around the group, nearing the only other person in front of her—a man that, from the backside, looked to be about her age, wearing slacks and a button-down. The activities building was in sight, and she was making a beeline toward it when the man abruptly changed directions and smacked right into her. The phone he held in one hand skittered to the wood chips under the shrubs at the edge of the path, and the coffee he held in his other hand smacked into her chest, spilling coffee all down her front.

Elise gasped at the force of the bump and the shock of the warm liquid suddenly covering her clothes.

"What were you—" the man said. "Why were you following so close?"

"I was hurrying," Elise managed to sputter.

The man picked his phone up from the ground, tilting it in the light to make sure it was okay. "Are you okay?" he asked, then gave a frustrated growl as he looked down at his crunched-up coffee cup like it was her fault that the cup was squished and all its contents were currently being worn by her.

Thankfully, the man's coffee wasn't nearly as hot as a normal person would've liked it. Still, though, this was going to make her so late for her meeting with Merit Casselman, and she was angry at the man's careless attitude about bumping into her.

She looked him up and down. With that face, that build, and that confident air that only came from owning a great deal of money, he was probably used to getting everything he wanted. Getting a man like that to feel anything for causing her to be late and getting coffee stains all over one of her favorite shirts was pointless. Getting mad about an accident was also pointless.

"I'm fine," she said. "Thank you for your concern. Now if you'll excuse me, I'm in a hurry."

As she speed-walked the rest of the way to the activities building, she shook off the encounter. She was working a job she loved at one of the most beautiful beaches in the world, and had a chance to earn everything she needed this summer. She wasn't about to let herself stop enjoying all that.

She grabbed a tub of wipes from the kids' activity area on her way into her office, closed all the blinds, and locked the door. After stripping off her t-shirt and shorts, she used the wipes to clean the beach off her arms and legs and the coffee off her stomach.

"The guy doesn't even put sugar in his coffee," she muttered as she tossed the dirty clothes in a bag, hoping they'd still be salvageable even if she didn't get to pre-soaking them until later. "Maybe that's why he was so annoyed."

Thankfully, as an activity director who worked with all ages doing all kinds of activities, she had learned long ago that it was important to keep a backup outfit in her office. So she at least had an option. She quickly pulled on a flowing blouse and some canvas shorts and then ran a brush through her hair, which had way more sand in it than she had expected.

Then she hurried to the clubhouse, a full seven minutes late, and as Quin was greeting a couple at the host's stand, Elise scanned the dining room for Merit. She wished she would've asked Graham for a picture, or Googled the guy or something. She got the sense from talking with Graham that Merit was probably somewhere around 45, but she didn't know anything about hair color, weight, build, or any of it. So she just looked for a man sitting alone, looking like he wasn't happy that she was late.

Her eyes landed on the man who had just spilled his coffee on her, sitting at a table with a brand new, fresh, black coffee in front of him. He must've desperately needed that coffee. Maybe if Quin led her to a table anywhere near him, she'd stop to suggest that a couple of sugars in that coffee might brighten his outlook.

When he returned from seating the couple, Elise said, "Good morning, Quin!"

He gave her a warm smile back. "It's not too often we're graced with your presence in the mornings."

"You're sweet," she said. "I'm meeting a man by the name of Merit Casselman. Has he checked in yet?"

"He has—let me lead you to him."

Three

MERIT

Nothing had gone right for Merit since yesterday when he left work and everything he had known for the past six years. When he got back to his office right after his meeting with Graham, he had brought up the company's numbers on his computer's monitor and had only been looking at them for two minutes when he lost the connection. He'd called IT, and they let him know that they had already flipped the switch, locking him out of the system.

He'd checked his phone—it was out there, too. And trying to convince Graham that he needed to look at everything once before he left made no difference.

But that hadn't stopped him from trying to get in through a back door during his five-and-a-half-hour flight and layover, or during the short drive from Myrtle Beach International to the resort.

Once he got checked in at the resort and was shown to a ridiculously large mansion on the beach, he got his laptop connected to the WiFi and tried to find a way into his company's internal database, since he couldn't get into the app itself. He was hoping to, at the very least, get into their scheduling app. Maybe if he could get his executives' schedules, he could see who they had meetings with, and at least get a sense of what was going on.

Out of the two of them, Graham was the coder. Merit was the businessman. Still, though, he'd picked up quite a bit of technical knowledge over the years. None of that knowledge helped, though. The only thing he could access was the website that anyone in the world could access.

Finally, at 3:00 a.m. South Carolina time, he gave up and glanced around the mansion for the first time. The driver had put his luggage in his bedroom—somehow he hadn't even noticed. There were three big suitcases. How much stuff had Carla thought he needed? After looking through the first two, he gave up trying to find pajamas and just stripped down to boxers and a t-shirt and collapsed into bed.

He had woken up feeling every bit of the time difference, the day of travel, the stress of not being able to get information, and the late night. And now, here he sat, bleary-eyed, at just after 7:00 a.m. Denver time, across from the woman who he had spilled his first cup of coffee on.

The least she could've done was gotten mad at him for it. Slapped him. Yelled. Demanded he pay her cleaning fees. Anything to make him justified in being angry at her for it. But no. She had to go and be kind and understanding. He was still angry at her for it.

He was already coming to the meeting not at his best,

and before they even got started, he had spilled coffee all down the front of the woman who held his fate in her hands.

"I didn't expect you to be this young," the woman said as she sat down.

And he didn't expect her to be young and radiant and beautiful. He expected someone more like Carla, he realized. This was actually kind of nice. He wasn't about to be a creeper and say that out loud, though.

People were always surprised at his age—that was nothing new. Her checking him out, though—that was also kind of nice.

"And I didn't expect you to be so forgiving of someone dumping coffee down their front."

She laughed, which made him smile. And that, for some strange reason, caused her to lean forward and peer into his cup of coffee. "I take it you added sugar this time?"

He shook his head, confused as to why she was asking. His eyes caught his phone, and he wondered again how he could get those numbers or that schedule. He cleared his throat. "I hear you're supposed to make me go do fun activities." He winced at the way "fun activities" came out. Like he didn't believe they could be fun. Truthfully, he didn't, but he hadn't meant for it to sound that way. "So what's on the calendar for us today?"

"Not so fast," she said. "We need to talk first, so I can see where you are at before I can choose the best thing. I'm not going to make a set schedule for the next four weeks; I'm going to decide as we go so we can do what seems best."

"You're the expert." He spread his arms wide. "Ask your questions."

"You seem a little hostile."

He didn't mean for it to be that obvious. "I apologize. Let's just say that if I had a choice in the matter, I wouldn't be here."

"You don't like visiting heaven on earth?"

He smiled at her earnestness. And her dimples—they were kind of cute. "Not when it takes me away from where I'm supposed to be."

She looked down at his hands, which suddenly made him feel self-conscious for some reason, so he laid one on top of the other on the table.

"I see that you keep reaching for your phone. What's on there that is pulling you to it?"

He let out a little growl. Was she supposed to be his psychiatrist now, too? Maybe that's what Graham should've signed him up for. He was hoping he could ignore the question, but she just patiently waited, with no judgment in her eyes, only curiosity. So he said, "Updates on my company."

"Tell me about the last time you weren't thinking about your company. What were you doing?"

He didn't answer. Partly because he didn't want to admit it to her, and partly because he couldn't remember the last time.

"Oh," she said like his thoughts had been written on his face. "Really? You think about it *all* the time? Last thing before you go to bed, first thing when you wake up in the morning?"

"Isn't that the way it is with anything you're passionate about?"

She shrugged. "I guess so. But let's talk about during the rest of the day. Do you think about your company while you're watching TV?"

"I don't watch TV."

"During a movie?"

"I don't go to movies."

"Okay, but what about other things? Do you think about it when you are on a date? Grocery shopping? Doing hobbies? Visiting family?"

He didn't want to tell her that he didn't do most of those things, and the things that he did do, he did while thinking about his company. So he just stayed silent.

"I see." She bit her lip, studying him. "Are you afraid of heights?"

"Nope."

"Claustrophobic?"

He shook his head. He wanted to tell her that he wasn't afraid of staring down a boardroom full of members who were twice his age and had MBAs and doctorate degrees, either. He was suddenly feeling very out of his element and wanted her to know that he wasn't just some punk kid whose business partner felt the need to tell him exactly what to do.

This was stupid. Graham sent him all the way out here, but it wasn't going to do any good. Hanging out in "heaven" with someone who was asking too many personal questions wasn't going to change anything.

The woman pulled a schedule out of her bag and opened it up, but didn't turn it so he could see. So he just watched as her eyes scanned through a few things. Then she gave a nod, closed the book, and looked back at him, a smile spreading across her face.

"Okay, I can see that it's not going to be easy to get you to stop thinking about your company when it is so much a part of your daily life. So it seems the first order of business is to do an activity where it's *impossible* to think about your company."

It's not that he thought about the same things all the time. He thought about the numbers often, sure. But when he wasn't thinking about that, he was thinking about market trends, sales techniques, marketing possibilities, employee incentives, new technology, or expanding, improving, growing, changing.

That she thought she could get him to stop thinking about all of it was actually kind of amusing. He smiled at her. "So you're telling me that we're going to go see a movie?"

She laughed, the sound joyful and uninhibited in a way he hadn't heard for a while. "Nope. We," she dragged out the word, "are going parasailing."

By noon, he had taken a golf cart back through the hilly trails leading to his mansion, changed into swim trunks, unpacked a little, and then taken the golf cart back to the main part of the resort. He was walking down to the docks to meet Elise when he got a phone call from Graham. He pressed to answer the call. "Hello?"

"Hey," Graham said. "I'm just calling to check-in. What do you think of the place?"

"It's pretty impressive."

"And what about that mansion you're staying in?"

"It's great. Big. And over the top. It's a whole lot of house for one person. It reminds me of the giant house I have at home that I don't utilize."

"You really would've been fine if I had rented one of the bungalows, wouldn't you?"

"I'd be fine even if I still lived in my college dorm."

Graham laughed. "Moving on then. You've met Elise, right?"

"We might've bumped into each other."

"And what do you think of her? She seemed pretty great when we video chatted."

"She's great, too."

"Dateable?"

"Graham." Merit didn't want to date anyone while he was here. And now that he knew that Graham wanted him to date Elise, she was especially off his list. "She's not." After a moment's pause, he asked, "How are sales doing? I'd love to hear just the new client numbers."

"Do you think you might be addicted to the dopamine hit you get from hearing the numbers?" Graham asked.

"This is my company too. I'm the CEO—knowing the numbers is my job. My responsibility. My right."

The phone was quiet for several moments, then Graham said, "Merit, I'm not just trying to make you my trained monkey here. This is all about you becoming the you that you and the universe deserve. The you that this company deserves."

"Thanks, Mom." When Elise waved at him from the dock, he waved back. "I've got to run. We're going to go feed the ducks or something." Then he pressed to hang up the phone and shoved it into his bag.

"Are you excited?" Elise asked him as they walked down the wooden planks of the docks.

He was still trying to shake off the phone call with Graham and could think of several things he'd rather be doing, but he was still able to answer truthfully. "Yeah, I am." It had been a while since he last did anything fun outside of work. Probably since their last executive retreat when they went to a ski resort in the Colorado Mountains.

They got onto the boat and Elise introduced him to Joel and Lennox, the two guys who were manning the ship. Then he and Elise both put on life jackets. Joel got behind the wheel, and Lennox started telling them about parasailing as they went further out from the shore, where the ocean was smoother.

"Just step into the harness," Lennox said as he held it by Merit's feet. He did as he was told and then the man pulled it up high enough to wrap a belt around his waist and through the latch on his life jacket. The whole thing felt like a diaper sagging down. But then the man had him sit and showed how the low straps behind his legs made a seat for him to sit on when they were in the middle of his thighs.

Then the man went to the back of the boat and ran the cords of the parachute through a framework, then pushed on some kind of release that let the parachute go back behind the boat, inflating as it flew backward. The round chute was a rainbow of colors, and as it burst fully open, he found himself getting excited. Not that he'd ever admit that to Graham. This was the kind of thing that he would have loved to do when he was younger. But back then, he never would've been able to afford an activity like this.

Now he had plenty of money but didn't have the time to go fly to a source of water, hire a parasailing boat, and then do something like this. He hadn't ever had both money and time together at the same time at any point in his life.

Lennox connected a horizontal bar to the parachute, then called Merit and Elise back to the deck. He had them both sit down facing the front of the boat, then connected the strap on either side of their harnesses to the bar, making Merit feel like he was sitting in a swing.

"Are you ready?" Lennox asked.

Elise looked at Merit, grinning, and he couldn't help but let her excitement wash over him. He grinned back and nodded.

"Alrighty, I'm going to let you out slowly and you'll begin to climb. Once you get to full height, I'll leave you up there for about fifteen minutes before I bring you back down. When I do, I can set you gently back on the deck, or I can dip your legs into the ocean before bringing you in. Which'll it be?"

"Dip us," Merit said. He'd never been out of the state of Colorado before he and Graham had started ZentCube, and although he'd had business meetings near the ocean before, he'd never actually put more than just his feet in it.

Lennox gave them an informal salute. Merit grabbed hold of the straps at his side that led up to the horizontal bar, then Lennox released the catch to let them start going out and up.

The initial pull jerked them backward and then their feet were dangling five feet above the water. The man continued to release more of the cord leading to the parachute, and with it, they made a smooth climb up higher above the ocean and further out from the boat.

The climb took his breath away, sometimes literally. They flew higher and higher until the boat was tiny. The wind rushed past his face and at first all he could do was to look down at the ocean below his dangling feet. All the waves barely made a texture change on the surface of the ocean and it spread out below him so far. He looked out to the east, where it disappeared into the sky from the curvature of the Earth, the color of the sky nearly blending seamlessly into the color of the ocean.

Up here felt free. The wind raced across his face, pulling them gently side to side, the height exhilarating, all of it coming together to make him feel like he was flying without actually having to do any of the work of flying.

Eventually, he managed to pull his gaze away from the

sky and ocean and to the shore. From this height, he could see the full sixty miles of beaches that made up the Grand Strand, many of them filled with people out soaking in the summer sun. Resorts dotted the beaches, and if he looked back behind them, he could see The Royal Palm, and even the palm tree-covered hills and paths leading to where he was staying. Even further inland, he could see the entire city, the SkyWheel standing tall and proud.

This was his first time in South Carolina, and although he was seated next to a window on the flight here, he realized that he hadn't looked out it even once. He had been so focused on trying to get information on his company that he had his nose buried in either his phone or his laptop the whole time. The car drive to the resort as well. If he had known what he was missing, he'd have made sure to look.

"Incredible, isn't it?" Elise asked.

He nodded, words failing him. It was one of the most incredible sights he had ever seen. One of the most incredible feelings he'd ever felt. This was the kind of thing he knew he'd remember for his whole life. The kind of thing that pulled people back to a location over and over. He was pretty sure he could come up here daily and never tire of it.

"Incredible" was definitely how he would describe it.

Four

ELISE

ELISE CLOSED her eyes and put her arms straight out, letting the wind hit her as they flew way above the ocean, soaking in every moment. When they had first gotten to the dock, Merit had been irritable and sour and she had wondered if she had chosen incorrectly after all.

But now, seeing him bask in the moment, she knew it was the right choice. He hadn't said a single word since they'd left the deck of the boat, but joy was emanating from his face —an expression she hadn't come close to seeing before this moment, and one she didn't think he was capable of making.

Much too soon, she felt the tug of the ropes from the boat below, and they started slowly making their way back down to the ocean. Like she always did when she went parasailing, she focused on the beaches as they got lower and could see people better—on being able to watch them from the side of the water's edge that she rarely got to see.

As they neared the boat, they both let out a primal scream as Lennox lowered them down into the water, their dangling feet breaking the surface of the cold ocean, the salty water splashing up to their faces. After having the sun on their legs up in the air, the shock of cold felt refreshing.

Then, with a jerk, they were back up in the air, being pulled toward the boat. As they neared, they both swung their feet, searching for purchase, until they touched down on the smooth deck and they stood, the harnesses no longer pulling them up.

Lennox released their straps, and Merit turned to her, a grin spread across his face. She knew this was the thing that would get him to stop thinking about work. Then he opened his mouth.

"First thing I do when I get back," he said, "is line up a retreat with my executives to go someplace where we can do this."

Elise threw her hands up in the air and climbed down the stairs to the seats to take her harness off. All Merit Casselman cared about was making money, and having her take him on activities like this was wasting both of their time.

Instead of being seated at their outdoor table at The Green Olive, the posh restaurant at the clubhouse, Elise waited for Merit at the host's podium and chatted with Declan, a guy who was about her age and had worked at the resort every summer since she had started.

"A lei for you," Declan said as he placed one of the leis around her neck. This early June luau was a guest favorite event at The Royal Palm, and tickets were hard to come by. How Graham had managed to get tickets for Merit and Elise was a mystery to her, but she'd take it.

Tiki torches were lit all around the outdoor area, the scent of the roasted Kalua pig and sweet grilled pineapple drifted over the tables, and luau music played over the speakers. Centerpieces with bright flowers and colorful drinks with little umbrellas sat on top of all the tables, a palm leaf placemat beneath each place setting.

"Are you twenty-five yet?"

Elise shook her head. "Not until next spring."

"So still just summer flings for you then?"

"You know it."

"I respect that you honor a promise made to a deceased parent. That's pretty cool of you." He reached a fist out to her.

She bumped it with hers. "Thanks, Declan. That's really sweet. Most people just don't get it."

"Oh I'm not saying I get it—there's no way I could go until twenty-five before getting into any serious relationship. But I do respect your choice. So, have you scoped out any potential flings yet?"

"I don't know—I think I have my hands full for a while. I might not even be able to manage that this summer."

"What about that guy you're waiting for? He's going to be here for a while, right?"

She raised an eyebrow.

Declan rolled his eyes. "Okay, okay, I know the whole 'no dating guests' rule. But don't tell me you haven't imagined it. I can speak for my gender when I say that he's one of the more attractive ones of us."

"On the outside, sure."

"Oh? No heart of gold on the inside?"

Elise lifted a shoulder in a shrug. "The only thing he cares about is his company and making money."

"And you don't want to even imagine dating a guy like that."

"If there's one thing my mom taught me—"

"Besides waiting until you are twenty-five to date anyone seriously," Declan interjected.

She nodded. "Besides waiting to date seriously, is that life's too short to spend it pursuing the wrong priorities."

He nodded, his eyes on something behind her. "Your 'gold on the outside' is here."

Elise turned around to see that Merit was heading up the pathway to the host's area, dressed in a white linen shirt, tan pants, and leather flip flops, his dark waves looking perfectly wind-blown, the hint of a five o'clock shadow, dark sunglasses shielding his eyes from the setting sun.

Her breath quickened and she swallowed. He was definitely gold on the outside. And dressed like that—well, if it wasn't for the "I'd rather be elsewhere" look on his face, he could be a model for resort brochures. Their business would probably double.

"I apologize for keeping you waiting," he said as he stepped up to her. "You look amazing."

She glanced down at her dress—as if she could've forgotten what she was wearing. The dress was equal parts sizzling and fun. She hadn't wanted to show up tonight looking sizzling, but she'd only had a few hours' notice about tonight and it was the only floral print dress she owned. And it felt perfect for a luau.

Declan led them to their table, which was one of the ones furthest from the host podium but closest to the short wooden platform that sat right on the beach that was used as a stage. Wow. Last-minute tickets and the best seats in the house to boot.

Like a gentleman, Merit tucked her chair in just a bit as she sat, then took his seat next to her. Then, *un*like a gentleman, he took his phone out of his pocket as he sat down and placed it face-up next to his silverware.

"We didn't get to talk much after the parasailing today," Elise said. "What did you think of it?"

"Oh, it was amazing," Merit said. "I wanted to go back up the minute we got back."

She smiled. So the guy could have fun.

Their waiter stopped by just then, introducing himself and handing them drink menus. "Do you already know what you'd like, or should I give you a few minutes to decide?"

Merit handed the menu right back and said, "Something virgin. Surprise me."

Elise lifted an eyebrow, impressed. So the guy could be spontaneous as well. She wouldn't have guessed that. She handed her menu back as well. "Same for me."

As the waiter walked away, Elise said, "Do you always have them decide on your drink for you?"

"Most places seem to have a drink that they're proud of, and more often than not, that's what they'll bring you. It takes the guesswork out."

She smiled. "Good to know."

"Plus, it's one less decision to make. There have been studies that show that people can only make a certain number of good decisions a day. I know CEOs who buy ten of the same outfits and treat them as their uniform. That way they don't have to waste a decision on clothing in the morning, freeing up one good decision that they can use for running their company."

So it hadn't been spontaneity after all.

After their waiter brought their drinks—Lava Flows, a beautiful frozen drink that looked like red lava was flowing up from the bottom—the wait staff started bringing around the feast, one item at a time. Soon, their plates were filled with Teriyaki Chicken, Mahi Mahi, Kalua Pua'a, Poi, Taro Rolls, grilled shrimp and pineapple skewers, and sweet rolls.

They were eating their dinners, enjoying the festiveness of the evening, and having pleasant enough conversation when Merit picked up his phone and went into his email and dragged to manually search for new emails. So it hadn't even been a notification that made him pick up his phone.

"Are you expecting an important email?" she asked and did an excellent job of not showing any annoyance if she did say so herself. It wasn't like they were there on a date.

He sighed and put his phone down, face down this time. "Just anything about my company. I'm not even getting chatter. They locked my work email account and it was my only email address, so I had to go out and create a brand new one yesterday. I'm not even getting spam."

Sometimes it was really easy to just see Merit as a wealthy businessman who was very successful but didn't care about people. And then he went and said something like that, and she suddenly saw him as a man who was feeling homesick for his entire world. Part of her just wanted to wrap her arms around him.

But the bigger part—the part that always wanted to be good at her job, and not just because there was a life-altering bonus attached to it—wanted to tell him to snap out of it and to quit looking for comfort, because making life changes meant you had to quit whining and be willing to get uncomfortable.

She was just opening her mouth to say something when the lights for the outdoor stage came on and a bare-chested, bare-footed Polynesian man, wearing nothing more than a headdress and a dance skirt with flax strands hanging from a belt, started shouting. More men, dressed the same, came rushing onto the stage, all shouting and posturing. Then the first guy chanted something, and all the others got into a similar position and shouted a chant back.

The Haka dancers were all broad-chested, muscular men, many with tattoos, and they danced and chanted, their chests, legs, and arms getting redder and redder from the slapping motions. Although she couldn't understand the words they were chanting, watching it made her sit straighter, her heart thumping, excitement coursing through her. From the corner of her eye, she saw Merit looking much the same.

After they exited the platform, eight Polynesian women filed onto the stage wearing bright pink hula skirts, tall head-dresses, coconut bras, and leis. Drums sounded from a group off to the side that she hadn't noticed before, and the dancers started dancing the hula, their arm motions fluid and graceful, their hips moving fast, shaking their grass skirts. Elise was mesmerized.

When the third group entered the stage—men wearing dance skirts with bunched up fabric, big wooden beads hanging around their necks and on their wrists, a band of leaves around their heads—doing a male warrior hula, move-ment at her side caught her attention.

She let out a frustrated breath when she noticed that Merit had grabbed his phone and was searching in a browser for information on his company. He was missing an incred-ible performance! And it wasn't like the dancers couldn't see him looking like he thought they were boring.

"Merit," she whispered just loud enough for him to hear over the drums. He immediately set the phone down, seeming embarrassed that he'd found it in his hand in the first place.

After the last group had performed, soft Hawaiian music began to play again over the speakers, and the wait staff started bringing out desserts. Elise turned to Merit.

"Merit, we need to talk." Okay, she probably should've started with different words; no one liked to hear those. He turned toward her, one arm resting on the table, and suddenly she just really wanted to help him. Not because of her job or the bonus—there was just something about him that drew her to him.

She cleared her throat and started again. "Graham explained what was at stake for you with this trip. There's a lot at stake for me, too. From what I can tell, what Graham is offering you is pretty important to you."

"It is."

"My job," she said, "is not to make you think a certain way, or to get you to do things you don't want to do or to get you over your addiction to information about your company." He visibly flinched when she said *addiction*. Maybe she should've used a different word. "My job is to help you to have fun. That's it."

Although, technically, her bonus was kind of asking her to do those other things, too. But her job as an employee at The Royal Palm was to be his personal activity director.

"I know you said yes to Graham's offer because you're here. But when you told Graham yes, I get the sense that you were saying yes to wanting the company shares that he was offering. I don't feel like you've said yes to doing what he was asking. That yes wasn't solid. You're not fully committed, because your mind is still back in Denver. If you're not dedicated to fully being here, present in the moment, then all of this is pointless. We're both wasting our time.

"So I'm asking you right now to commit to this trip. Are you willing to *be* here fully? To immerse yourself in whatever activity we're doing?"

For a very long moment, he met her eyes, thinking, pondering, deciding, figuring things out. Elise kept her eyes on his, searching for the spark that told her this was possible. And then she saw it, a moment before he did. A smile spread all through her insides that she tried to keep beneath the surface until he finished deciding.

With his eyes still on hers, he said, "I'm not used to this. It won't be easy."

"Change never is. But I'm determined to see it through to the end if you are."

Then he gave a very decisive nod. "Okay, deal."

Instead of shaking his hand, she reached out and wove her fingers into his, like they were about to arm wrestle, and then threw their fists high in the air. What they needed more than a deal was a determination to be victorious.

Five

MERIT

YESTERDAY before the luau had been rough. Merit had spent thirty minutes on the phone with Carla, trying to get her to bend on any of Graham's rules, but she stood firm. It was one of the reasons why Merit had hired her as his assistant in the first place, but it was pretty frustrating when he was on the other side of it.

But today he was proud of himself. After the luau last night, he stuck his phone in his pocket and didn't even touch it until after he was back at his mansion. He even got ready for bed before he opened his phone to set his alarm. And of course to see if any emails had come in, just in case.

And after he turned off his alarm this morning, he didn't touch it again until he was in the gym on the bottom floor of the mansion, and that was only to turn on his music. He thought Elise would probably be just as proud of him as he was.

Having a healthy mind was very important to Merit, and

he knew that part of keeping it healthy was to keep his body healthy, so that wasn't something he ever slacked on.

He even had a gym installed on the ground floor of the main building at ZentCube so that all of his employees could easily get in some gym time on their lunch hour or before or after work, without adding travel time to their day. It had come with the added benefit of him and all of his employees being able to chat more casually with each other, forging bonds that might not be there otherwise.

As he used the weight machine, a sudden loneliness hit him, and he realized how much he missed his morning workout chats with his employees. Graham was his best friend and by far the person in the world he talked to most often. He missed their chats, but he also wasn't very happy with Graham right now and didn't want to talk with him.

But he did want to talk to his Chief Financial Officer, Talene. Her son had planned to propose to his girlfriend last night. She had told him all about it on Monday, and he was wondering how it went. If he'd been back at ZentCube, he would have found out while they were both at the gym this morning. He walked over to his phone and called her.

"Merit!" she said, sounding excited that he called. "How is the vacation? I hear the beaches there are gorgeous. Please tell me they're gorgeous."

He hadn't been on the beach yet. But he had seen them while parasailing, so he told her about the view.

"That's it. I'm spending my next vacation at The Royal Palm."

"You should. But I'm warning you right now, the

humidity may try to kill you. So how did the proposal go? That was last night, right?"

Talene gave him a detailed rundown of how her son went to a fancy restaurant with a wishing fountain, and they each threw in coins and made wishes and then he got down on one knee. Talene, her husband, and their daughter had been hiding behind some shrubs by a bench and secretly filmed the whole thing so they could have it playing at their wedding. The whole time they talked back and forth, Merit felt the stress leaving him, and happiness taking its spot. He started feeling like himself again.

After Talene's story, he asked how the financial numbers were looking, since that was always the natural progression of their conversations.

"I would love to shoot the breeze with you about anything, Honey," Talene said, "but you know I'm not going to give you any company information."

He hadn't even thought too much about it before he asked, but as soon as he had gotten the *no* from her, all the happiness that he'd been feeling fled, and before he knew it, he had called six of his seven chief officers—all of them except Graham. None of them would tell him anything. Each time he hung up, he found himself feeling more desperate for crumbs. Not even the IT people, the building receptionist, or the managers he often chatted with would give him anything.

After going back up to his room, he chucked his phone on his bed and got in the shower. As the hot water washed over him, he thought of the earnestness he had seen in Elise's eyes the night before. That willingness to help that promised to not judge him, but to push him regardless. He had felt such peace as he met her eyes and committed to her to have fun. His conversation with Talene, once it had switched from personal to business, along with every call after that, had definitely not been fun.

This was a setback, he told himself. But it didn't mean he wasn't still moving forward. He had made a promise to a girl, after all.

Elise hadn't said what they were going to be doing on the beach, but he decided to wear swim trunks to be on the safe side. He pulled on a snug t-shirt and slipped into his flip flops, and then went outside to the man in the golf cart who had been sent to pick him up.

He found Elise at the Royal Palm's main beach area, which already had quite a few families with blankets spread and shade umbrellas raised. Elise, though, was near a bunch of kids who all looked like they were between the ages of seven and thirteen or so, who were all making sandcastles.

"Hi," she said, a bright smile lighting up her face. Her eyes seemed to have magic in them when she was on the beach, and he felt himself being pulled to her.

Another woman, a couple of years younger than Elise and a few inches shorter, and a little darker skinned, who seemed to be running the activity with the kids, stepped up next to Elise and looked him up and down. "Well, hello salty goodness." She stuck her hand out. "I'm Zabrena. I'm guessing you're Merit Casselman?"

He shook her hand, hoping that his awkwardness wasn't visible. He wasn't exactly used to being in places where people unabashedly flirted with him. "Nice to meet you."

"Zabrena," Elise said, a warning note in her voice, an eyebrow raised, "shouldn't you be hanging out with the kids?"

"She loves me," Zabrena said, "even when it sounds like she doesn't."

"You know I do," Elise said back, chuckling. Then she turned to Merit. "Are you ready for a morning spent soaking up the sun?" She was wearing board shorts that made her legs look long and lean, over a blue-striped one-piece swimsuit that brought out the blue in her blue-green eyes.

He met her smile with one of his own. "Yep—where are we headed?"

"We're staying right here."

He looked around, confused.

"Today is sandcastle creations day, and you, Merit, are going to make a sandcastle with me."

A flash of nervousness hit him. He didn't know the first thing about making sandcastles, and most of the kids here were making some pretty impressive ones. He didn't want to create a stupid one that would just keep falling down while they showed him up. Still, though, he took a seat on the sand near Elise when she sat down by a pile of supplies. "Did you bring me here to take me down a few notches?"

Elise laughed a big, appreciative laugh and pointed at

him with a yellow plastic shovel. "I am not your psychologist, remember? I'm here to help you have fun, so that's exactly what we're going to do. When was the last time you made a sandcastle?"

She started using her shovel to level out the sand in front of them, so he picked up the blue shovel and started doing the same. "Never."

"For real?"

"I grew up in Pueblo, Colorado, where beaches in any direction were a million miles away. We were dirt poor, too, so we didn't go on vacation. We did have a teeny little lake, though—Lake Minnequa—but it didn't exactly have sandy beaches."

"Well, then, you're in for a treat. One that will bring out your inner nine-year-old. Let me ask you this: when was the last time you created something that wasn't for work?"

She was probably taking his silence as an unwillingness to answer her question, but the truth was it was just taking him a while to remember back that far. "Back on the University of Denver campus, my friends Ian, Saint, Noah, and Graham and I all made a music video where we serenaded a girl to ask her to a dance."

He chuckled at the memory. It was a stupid video where they hadn't cared about what people thought—they just did what they thought was funny and cheesy and hoped that the girl did, too.

"So, like six or seven years ago?"

He nodded. "About that."

"You don't have any hobbies?"

"Not that aren't related to work. I really do spend all of my waking hours on it. It seems pointless to have hobbies that aren't going to get me anything."

"Merit."

He looked up at her, and she started filling a plastic castle mold with somewhat wet sand. "Hobbies are important precisely because they don't get you anything. Once you start using them for something, they either become work or something that's judged for its value, which takes away some of the fuel your creative self gets by doing them."

Merit was filling his third bucket with sand—apparently, the water content in the sand made a big difference in how well it would hold together. He carefully tipped this one over and voila! It looked perfect. He started filling it up a second time from the same area. "I guess I just don't see the point. Maybe not everyone needs that."

"Everyone does. And the more you fill your creative well by doing things that *won't* be judged, the more you'll be able to draw from that well and spend it on the things that *will* be judged. It's like putting money in a bank account so you can spend it later. Or eating so you'll have energy. Or sleeping so later you can be awake. If you want to come up with creative solutions to problems, you have to first fill that well by doing creative things."

Merit just shoveled in silence, thinking about what she was saying.

After a few moments, Elise said, "So, to answer your question, I brought you here today to remind you what it's like to create something just for the fun of it—not because it's going to make you money. Just creativity for the sake of creativity." She gestured at the group of kids who were all building their own sandcastles. "Kids understand the importance of it; we forget."

The more they worked on their castle, the more fun he found himself having. Together they had built a castle with a bunch of different levels, and they had carved doors and windows into it. They had even made a moat around the outside of the castle, and he was trying to figure out if there was a way to make a drawbridge that would go over the moat.

"Do you want castle walls around it? I can start making it for you."

Merit looked up from where he was working to see a kid who was probably eight or nine standing near their castle, a plastic shovel in one hand and a smaller mold that looked like a castle wall in the other. "Sure! Do you want to start over here?"

The boy sat down and went to work. It wasn't long before three more kids joined them, all working together to help make their castle even larger. Maybe if enough of them ended up coming over, they could make it gigantic.

He looked at Elise when he felt her gaze on him. She was watching him with an expression that was part curious and part something else that he couldn't name, but made heat spread through his torso. Their legs were both covered in sand from sitting in it, and their hands were pretty covered, too. She had her hair pulled back into a ponytail, but she still had some sand in it. A little was on her sun-pinked cheek, too, where she must have scratched it.

If advertising agencies wanted to sell clothing or sunscreen or makeup or shampoo, this was what they should advertise. A woman sitting in the sand, exercising creativity by building a sandcastle, not caring what the people around her thought. Before this moment, he never would've thought it would be so attractive.

He had been so wrapped up in his business for so long that he hadn't realized how much he missed this feeling. If he had been looking for someone to date, he wouldn't have to go any further than Elise.

But of course, he wasn't looking. This wasn't real life here. This was just for four weeks, then he'd head back into his life where he couldn't lose focus by dating. There just wasn't time for it. His business would probably eventually get to the point where there would be time, but right now wasn't it.

No, right now he needed to stop being distracted by the beautiful woman working next to him and finish building the north tower. Then he, Elise, and the army of kids surrounding them would need to decide if they should go up or out with their castle expansion.

He didn't know how long they had worked, but the sun had moved quite a bit, his skin felt heated to his core, and his stomach was growling. When they finished their rather impressive castle, the nine of them who had been working on it—which now even included Zabrena—all stood in a row, admiring their work.

Merit realized that he was standing with his chest out, shoulders back, arms akimbo, and he felt great. This was one of the most impressive things he had made in a very long time. Something that hadn't existed before. A real, tangible, touchable something that he helped to create.

It was also something temporary. When the tide came in, the castle would be washed away. That didn't matter, though. Making it felt like a gift, and he got to keep that.

"You," Zabrena said, placing a hand on his shoulder, "do good work. Now if you'll excuse me, I've got a bunch of kids to round up and get back to their parents."

As she walked off, Elise started brushing the sand off her legs. Then she looked out toward the ocean. "Do you want to go for a dip? We can wash the sand off and cool down our skin."

"Yeah, I do." Merit took off his shirt and tossed it on top of his bag. Then Elise grabbed his hand and raced out toward the water's edge.

Six

ELISE

As THEY RACED toward the ocean, Elise thought about how she had never been more proud of a human before. It was after one, which meant they had been working on the sandcastle for over three hours. She wondered if Merit realized that during that entire time, he hadn't pulled his phone out of his bag once. From what she had seen, he hadn't even put a hand toward his pocket where it normally was, or glanced at his bag like he was thinking about it. He hadn't even talked about business once.

The moment her feet hit the cool water, her whole body rejoiced. The further they ran in, their steps slowed by the water, the more energized and refreshed she felt. When the water got up to her mid-thigh, she dove into the next wave, submerging her body in the ocean, feeling its cooling effects over her entire body at once. She swam underwater until she needed to come up for a breath, then surfaced and stood, the water coming up almost to her chest.

A moment later, Merit surfaced near her, and they both crouched down to their shoulders, letting the waves rock them back and forth. She started rubbing her arms to get the more stubborn sand off. "So, what did you think of making the sandcastle?"

"Kudos on the choice. Well played."

Elise leaned back in the water, floating. "The water always feels so good after spending so long in the sun. One without the other can be a little miserable, but together, it's heaven."

She noticed that Merit started floating on his back, too, and for a couple of minutes, they just floated until the next wave would come and knock them into the water, then they'd float again until the next big one came.

Between the sand and the ocean, she knew they likely didn't have any sunscreen left on them, so she stood up, and Merit did right after, then she started leading them back toward the shore.

"We should probably go get some lunch. I can take us to the showers in the locker rooms by the pool if that works for you, so we can get cleaned up. Then I figured we would head over to the Mini Palm. There are always a lot of single ladies who hang out there—it would be a good place to find you a date."

"A date?" He shook his head. "I don't plan to date while I'm here."

She was going to have to work hard for this bonus. And he just happened to be a guy who was used to being the boss, not to people bossing him around. "It's my job to have you do a broad range of activities. Dating is one of them."

He shook his head. "A different activity will be just fine."

"Nope—dating is the activity. You'll just have to get your flirt on." She chuckled when she saw that the look on his face looked pretty much like the one she wore in the fifth grade when she was up on stage at her school's spelling bee and was asked to spell *conscientious*. She clapped a hand on his back and said, "Relax, hot stuff. Whether you're a little rusty or not, you're going to have no problem at all."

Elise spent enough time at the beach that she was a pro at showering and re-getting ready at any time during the day. She had gotten the entire process—showering, getting dressed, putting on moisturizer, lipstick, and mascara, and blow-drying her hair—down to twenty-one minutes flat. She even beat Merit out of the locker rooms, so she pulled out her phone and checked in on the group chat with her staff.

Zabrena, of course, complained about The Royal Palm's rule that said staff couldn't date guests and wondered about possibly setting up her older sister with Merit. HallieMae was out on a bike ride with the teens, and Kale was just heading over to the main building to check on the decorations for the Midsummer Ball.

When Merit met her outside, she slipped her phone into her bag and stood up. As she led them down the meandering path toward the Mini Palm, the outdoor restaurant with gourmet burgers and fries, Merit said, "I talk to women. I do. Three of my seven executive officers are women. My assistant is a woman. More than half of my top-level managers are women. But—" He reached a hand up and scratched the back of his neck.

She could tell how uncomfortable he was even trying to tell her, so she finished the sentence for him. "But you only talk to them about business stuff. You don't flirt on a regular basis."

"Right. I mean I *do* date occasionally."

"When your company has an evening event, and a plus one is expected."

He hesitated and then nodded.

"But it wasn't always like this. You were a pro at flirting back in college. You just forgot how over the past six years."

He gave her a look of surprise. "How did you know all that?"

"I know you knew how to flirt because you even made a music video to serenade a girl. Your mind wasn't always all consumed by business. You enjoyed yourself back then and had fun with your friends. And," she motioned to all of him, "you look like this. It's not hard to figure out that you did well in the dating department in college. Just tap into your inner twenty-year-old."

She led him up to the opening in the low fence and the host seated them near the outdoor bar, where a group of women in their early twenties sat drinking fruity drinks and laughing. Their waiter, Landon, came over a few minutes later to give them their menus.

Merit glanced at it for a moment, and then asked, "What do you recommend?"

"My favorite is the Mushroom Bacon Swiss Burger, but another guest favorite is the BBQ burger."

Merit handed the menu back. "Your favorite sounds good. I'll take that with fries and a Coke."

"And I'll have the Steak and Everything with onion rings and water." She nodded toward the women at the bar. Landon was a single college student, so they were probably pretty close to his age. She was sure they had been on his radar. "How long have those women been there?"

Landon glanced over. "About an hour. Why?"

"Merit here needs a date. Which one do you think's the most dateable?"

Landon looked at Merit, and Merit looked like he might be blushing. But she saw the bro exchange between the two men and the slight nod from Merit that it was okay to proceed. "Long, light brown hair with the blue shirt and jeans."

Elise flashed him a smile. "Thanks, Landon."

He brought their drinks a moment later and their food, thankfully, not too long after that. Elise was always starving after spending hours on the beach. She took a huge bite of her sandwich.

Merit picked up his burger and looked at it, then nodded toward the women at the bar and said, "I don't even know what to do," before taking a bite.

Elise swallowed, then dabbed her lips with a napkin and said, "Well, you could go talk to them." She glanced in the direction of the women and saw that they had noticed Merit. "Or, you could finish eating because I know you must be starving, and we can just go from there."

She took another bite of her sandwich and heard her phone buzz with the text tone she had set for her staff. She pulled it out of her bag and looked at the notification—it was a text from Kale.

> KALE: The decorations are a disaster! How soon can you come to the main building?

She opened the text and typed back, *I'll be there in five.* Then she slid it back into her bag. "I have to run and deal with a problem one of my team is having." At the panicked look on Merit's face, she said, "Don't worry—I'll be your wingman before I leave."

Elise went up to the outdoor bar, making sure to lean in right next to the woman Landon had pointed out as most datable, then called out to where he was refilling someone's soda. "Hey, Landon, I've got to run. Will you grab me a takeout box when you get a second?" Then she waited right where she was.

The woman glanced down at Elise's hand, probably checking for a wedding ring, then said, "So, um, are you and that guy you were sitting with together?"

Elise shook her head regretfully. "I wish. I'm the activities director here and he's a guest, so it's against the rules. It's too bad because he's a great guy."

The two of them turned to look at Merit at the same time. The other woman said, "Strong, too."

Yep. Those thoughts had gone through Elise's head, too, when he had first taken off his shirt, and even more so when she had clapped her hand on his bare back in the ocean. But, as she'd said, he was against the rules, even if she was willing to date casually.

Landon handed her the to-go box and she thanked him. Then she said to the woman, "Hey, I just got called away unexpectedly, and I feel bad ditching him in the middle of our lunch. He mentioned earlier that he thought you were cute. How would you feel about keeping him company while he finishes? Then I wouldn't have to feel so bad about leaving."

The woman looked like she had been hoping to talk to Merit, and seemed plenty happy to have the opportunity wrapped up in a bow and handed right to her. "I can do that."

"Thank you," Elise said. "His name's Merit."

She walked back over to the table and put her sandwich and onion rings in the container. "Okay, she's coming over as soon as I leave. The scary part's done, so just chat with her, preferably about something other than your company, and then if things go well, ask her if she wants to go out tonight. I'll text you a list of date ideas as soon as I can."

Merit nodded. "Got it."

"Channel your inner twenty-year-old."

"Channeled."

She placed a hand on his arm, which felt way too nice—she was going to have to stop doing that. "You've got this."

When she got to the main building, Kale was in the back where they kept event decorations, amid several boxes of twinkle lights, all strewn about, overwhelm and defeat all over his face.

"What happened?" she said as she walked into the room, trying to take in what she was seeing.

"The shelf above it had some kind of structural flaw and couldn't hold the weight that was put on it, so the contents of that shelf all came crashing down onto this one. The bulbs are all smashed. I've checked—there's maybe one strand that might be okay, but I haven't found it yet."

Elise carefully stepped through the mess and peeked into the boxes. Shattered glass lay amongst all the cords. "Does Devin or Cyree know yet?"

"Devin does," Kale said as he pulled another strand out of an open box, shaking the broken glass from it. "He said he'll get more ordered so they'll be here in time."

"Oh good."

"But he also said you're in hot water for not having approved the budget for the activities six weeks ago."

Elise winced.

"And for not responding to the emails he had sent about other things over the past few days. And apparently, there are a few guest emails to you that have gone unanswered as well. And he was saying something about the guest numbers and expense numbers spreadsheet not being updated."

She grimaced. He had probably sent her emails about that, too. Office work was the part of her job that she was the worst at. The fun parts were all flashy and calling to her nonstop, which made it easy to ignore the rest. And then she'd gone and hired a full staff of people just like her— people who would have a great time interacting with the guests, but who would rather go to the dentist than be cooped up in an office putting numbers into spreadsheets on a computer.

Normally, she forced herself to do office work for a few hours on Wednesdays after their team meetings, whether she liked it or not, but this week she'd gone straight to meeting Merit. No wonder Devin was on the warpath.

The next time she hired a new person, she decided she didn't care how easily they could take charge of an event and ensure its success—all she cared about was if they thought the most exciting parts of the job were the ones that Elise found the most mind-numbing.

"Well, I guess I know what I'll be doing for the next several hours."

"Go," Kale said, motioning for her to vacate the room. "Take those doom-and-gloom paperwork thoughts far away from here. I'll get this all taken care of."

Elise walked back to the activities building, soaking in the sun and fresh air while she could, before heading in to be cooped up in a joyless room for the rest of the day.

Seven

MERIT

MERIT WOKE up feeling like he'd been hit by a train, so he slept in until seven Denver time, which was nine Myrtle Beach time, making him feel like a complete slacker. But he wasn't meeting Elise until two today, and it wasn't like he had board meetings or client meetings or planning meetings to go to.

So he got up and went for a run on the beach and up and down the hilly area around his and the other rental mansions, loving the difference in how it felt to run at sea level versus how it felt to run in a city where the elevation was a mile above sea level. Here, he practically had super-powers. All he needed to do was to learn how to breathe air that was so humid.

When he got back to his place, he lifted weights in the gym and in between reps, got a text from Graham.

> GRAHAM: Elise told me you went on a
> date last night. I'm impressed! What's
> her name? Is there photographic
> evidence? Because I'm not sure I'm
> going to believe it until I see it.

He shook his head. He had only agreed to the date because he knew Graham well enough to know that he could very easily throw in a stipulation to date, so he figured he might as well not fight Elise on it. Knowing Graham well enough to know he'd ask for a picture was also the reason why he had taken one at the restaurant. He added the picture to a text and responded.

> MERIT: Piper, and remember that one
> time in college when we took Noah's
> jeep up in the mountains and fell into
> that ravine?

> GRAHAM: Oh. Crashed and burned that
> badly, huh?

> MERIT: It's safe to say there won't be a
> second date. We didn't even finish the
> first date.

Merit did a dozen reps on the chest press, waited thirty seconds, did a dozen more, and then picked up his phone to see Graham's response.

> GRAHAM: What went wrong?

MERIT: The conversation was only about her and a class where she had a crush on the professor, we found nothing in common, and she was awful to the wait staff.

GRAHAM: Table Yelper?

MERIT: She even said her review out loud—very loud—as she was typing it in.

But our server was great.

GRAHAM: So you over-tipped to compensate?

MERIT: Added an extra zero to the end and wrote an apology.

Piper thought we should stiff the guy.

Merit shook his head and went to the lat pulldown machine. He didn't hear a response buzz from a text, so he kept working out. His conversation with Graham was going pretty well, and it felt as though things were closer to normal between them. It made him wonder if he could get him to share a tidbit about how the company was doing. They were holding off going public—a decision that he was regretting now—which meant he couldn't even look at stock prices to give him a clue that things weren't going downhill in his absence.

He moved on to the seated row, and it wasn't until he

finished with that machine that he heard the buzz from his phone.

> GRAHAM: Keep trying. I'm sure there are other women there you will connect with.

> MERIT: If I come across someone, sure.

> GRAHAM: Don't just wait for something to happen—go out searching and find someone. It's exactly the kind of attitude you used to grow this company so quickly, and it's what you need to do now to find a great date.

> MERIT: I'm not looking to find a great date.

> GRAHAM: Do it anyway. But this time, try to converse with them a little more first.

Merit rolled his eyes and tossed his phone onto the padded seat of the rowing machine. Then he picked up the phone again and read Graham's last text. *Try to converse with them a little more first.* "Converse" wasn't a very Graham-like word—he would've used "chat."

Then a memory hit him. Back in college when they had first started creating their company, before Graham had graduated and Merit had dropped out so they could work on it full time, Graham had told him that he changed his password daily—a by-product of being a computer science major who focused heavily on data security—and it took work to remember it when it changed so often. With it on his mind more, he said he kept finding himself using the word in regular conversation instead of using the word he normally would.

Could *converse* be his password? Merit had never even desired to log in as Graham before, but that would give him access to the calendar and schedules since all executives could access them. It could maybe even get him a few numbers from the app if Graham had email alerts set up. He raced upstairs and opened his laptop, then tried logging in to the company site with Graham's login name and every combination of numbers and letters that spelled *converse* that he could come up with.

He knew a seventh try would lock him out and Graham as well, so after the sixth try got him nowhere, he gave up.

For today.

From now on, though, he was going to start paying more attention to any out-of-character words that Graham said or texted. Somewhere along the line, he'd figure out the right one.

While he waited for two o'clock to roll around, Merit got lunch and explored more of the resort and chatted with lots of people who worked at the resort and who were there as guests, just like he did as he was doing his daily walk-through of his building. It made him almost feel like he was back in a routine again.

The more he walked around, the more his thoughts kept returning to Elise and to that smile that radiated genuine happiness. He enjoyed being around her. She stood up to him as an equal and didn't take any bull from him. He had been a CEO for long enough to experience plenty of people who only told him what he wanted to hear, so he'd learned to greatly appreciate candor in a person.

Merit met Elise at the Surf Shack at two, just like they had planned. He was learning to just go with the flow since she was making a habit of not letting him know ahead of time what they would be doing. Today, the only instruction she had given him was to wear closed-toe shoes. So when he saw that she was wearing shorts, a tank top, sunglasses, and a hat, he felt like he'd made the correct choice when he'd chosen light-colored canvas shorts and a light blue t-shirt.

He smiled when she looked in his direction and waved him over.

The Surf Shack was filled with rental equipment—not just for surfing, but with everything imaginable for the beach. "Merit, I would like to introduce you to Jax. He runs the surf shop, and pretty much knows everything there is to know about everything on the beach."

Jax chuckled. "If nothing else, I'm good at making things up. Elise tells me that you two are going to rent some skateboards and take a trip down the boardwalk."

Merit raised his eyebrows. So that's what the plan was.

"There's a lot to see on the boardwalk," Elise said. "It's something you can't skip if you're coming to Myrtle Beach.

It's only a bit more than a mile long, so walking it isn't bad at all, but I figured that skateboarding would be more fun." She grinned at him, and some of her excitement spilled in his direction.

Jax handed them over some skateboards and they carried them under their arms until they reached the wooden walkway. The pathway was wide, and wooden railings ran along the sides a good portion of the way. All of it went right along the edge of the ocean.

They put the skateboards down and stepped onto them. This was actually an activity that Merit had done before. He hadn't owned a bike, but he did get practically everywhere on a skateboard. He even took one to college and rode it all over campus to get between classes that weren't close.

He pushed off and put both feet on the skateboard, feeling the vibration of the wheels on the wooden planks. The feeling brought him instantly back to his entire life before ZentCube. "I don't think I've ridden a skateboard since college!"

He glanced over and saw that Elise wasn't quite as steady and confident on hers, so he put a foot down, coming to a stop. "Whoa. Is this something I'm more experienced at here than you are?"

Elise came to a stop, too. "Okay, truth be told, I haven't ridden one of these for a couple of years. And even then, I haven't done it much. But I figured it would be easy."

"Don't worry," Merit said, putting out his hand. "You'll be a pro by the time we're done."

Elise gave him a "thank you" nod and grabbed his hand.

Hers was smooth and cool in his, and he was surprised at how great it felt to hold. He let her take the lead on how fast to go, and he just worried about being a steady support for her. It didn't take long before she was seeming a bit more confident on it.

"Do you come to the boardwalk often?"

Elise nodded. "At least every couple of weeks or so. Just not on skateboards. Obviously. But I've seen a lot of kids riding skateboards on it, and they always look like they're having so much fun."

It was fun. The breeze against his skin, the smell of the ocean, the familiar feel on his feet, Elise's hand in his—it was an intoxicating mix. The view wasn't bad, either. The ocean spread out on their right, with tons of shops and activities and performers and crowds on their left.

"You're pretty good."

"You should see me when I'm trying to show off."

"And I take it you did that a lot as a kid?"

"Some. It wasn't until college that I really gained confidence, though. There was this place on campus called Campus Green—"

"Right by Sturm Hall, right?"

Merit's eyes flew to Elise. "You know it?"

"I went to the University of Denver, too."

Merit put his foot onto the boardwalk, stopping his skateboard, not thinking about the fact that he was still holding Elise's hand, and made her step off her skateboard. "Where did you grow up?"

"Nestled Hollow, so not far from where you grew up. I

mean it was probably a two-and-a-half-hour drive, but when you consider the whole country, it's not far. It's just a little town in the mountains."

"I've heard of it."

Merit looked at her with new eyes. "Huh. Even on the other side of the country, I guess fellow Coloradans seek each other out unknowingly."

Elise hopped back on her skateboard and they started moving forward again. "Well, technically, I knew where you were from since Cyree first proposed Graham's plan. And Cyree sent him the bios of me and my staff at the beginning of their negotiations so he could choose who he wanted to be your activities director, so it looks like he's the one who chose the fellow Coloradan."

"So did you do an internet search for me when he told you I was from Colorado?"

"Nah," she said, waving him off. "I just figured you were some boring businessman. Did you Google me?"

"No—I just figured you were some boring activities director." She swatted at him, and he swerved away before coming back. He was enjoying this playful banter with her. "So, did you always know you wanted to be 'some boring' activities director?"

"Not until high school graduation. What about you? Did you always want to be a 'boring businessman?'"

"Yep. Well, the boring part is up for debate. But being an entrepreneur is in my blood. My dad ran his own business, my grandpa did, and my great-grandpa did. I opened my first one when I was eleven. It was a car washing service, and I advertised that I would come to you, so you didn't even have to leave home. Then I got there on my trusty skateboard, a bucketful of cleaning supplies in my hands."

They turned off the wooden boardwalk, and onto a paved walkway, where some street performers were dancing. "What brought you all the way out here?"

She shrugged. "Denver doesn't exactly have an ocean."

He knew a non-answer when he heard one. He decided to push further, to see if he could get her to say more. "But why South Carolina? California has an ocean and it isn't as far."

Elise just slowed her skateboard, looking out across the ocean, and didn't answer. There was more to her answer, and he suddenly very badly wanted to know it all.

ELISE

ELISE SPOTTED the flashy candy store she loved to go to and said, "Follow me!" It was a spot she wanted to show him, but more than that, she was hoping that all the bright colorful displays in the store would make him forget trying to understand why she came to Myrtle Beach. It was personal, and she didn't tell many people.

And for a bit, the store very much distracted him. They both picked up their skateboards and went inside, exploring all the round displays that went from floor to ceiling in a colorful, sugary explosion. They walked near a display of giant marshmallow bunnies.

"Let me guess," Merit said. "You had to get far away from Colorado because you were caught drunk driving and lost your license, and you really like to drive."

Elise laughed out loud. "I don't drink. Plus, I prefer a bike, or walking, or running. Or bus. Or kayaking."

"I've got it—you like the earlier time zone. It makes you

feel superior to know that you're waking up before the rest of the nation."

She chuckled and shook her head, then meandered toward the candy sushi. This playful side of Merit was rather enjoyable. She wondered if he was this way all the time when he was back home, being the CEO of ZentCube, or if it was just because he got some distance from the company.

"You're allergic to the cold. You can't stand being surrounded by feet of snow and want mild winters. Sand over snow."

"I miss the snow. It's not easy to make a sand snowman. I've tried."

"You prefer to drink your air."

She laughed. "Yeah, the humidity in Colorado is a bit different than it is here. You do get used to it, though. But no, not the reason."

"You need the sun to rise on the ocean, not set on it."

"As long as it's beautiful, I don't have a preference. Oh! Lollipops! We should get one. You know—since we've already gone back to your childhood with the skateboards." She led him to the display.

"You were getting away from a bad relationship. Your ex-boyfriend was a stalker, and the only way you could get away from him was to change your name and move seventeen hundred miles away."

She snort-laughed. "Not it."

"The stalker part or the getting away from an ex-boyfriend part?"

"Both. I promised my mom that I wouldn't get in a

serious relationship until I was twenty-five, so no ex-boyfriends to escape from." Elise leaned in to see what flavor a pink and purple one was.

"Huh." Merit paused a moment. "And she still holds you to that?"

"*I* hold me to it," Elise said. "*I'm* the one who made the promise."

"Ahh. A woman of integrity. I like it." And then he looked at her in a way that made her wonder if he liked *her*. "How old are you now?"

"Twenty-four and three months."

He stopped asking questions and started looking at the different flavors of suckers. "Maple bacon? In a sucker? That's just wrong."

They looked in silence for a few more minutes. Then, partly to take the focus off her, partly because she was curious, and partly because she needed to stop noticing how great it felt to be standing so close to him and do her job, she said, "So how was your date last night?" He picked up a banana raspberry sucker. "Terrible—thanks for asking."

"Then we need to find you a better someone for the next date."

"There's not going to be a next date."

"Merit, I can help you find someone."

"I know—you helped me find the last someone."

"I can help you find someone *good*."

He turned to her and let out a long sigh. "Listen, Elise. I know you've got good intentions. I will do all the activities

Graham wants me to do, but I don't want to add something else to the mix. Doing the activities is more than enough."

Elise's stomach sank. How was she going to get this man to go on five dates while he was at the resort? Graham wanted them to be dates that Merit enjoyed so that it would change his opinion on dating. That wasn't going to happen if he didn't actively participate in the finding of dates.

"Merit."

"No." He put the sucker back and grabbed a different one.

"You need to date."

"Tell me why."

She led them over to a mechanical display of gumballs that were being taken through a maze. "Because this entire trip is about you finding fun again. Doing things you haven't been doing. Trying new things. Enjoying life. Dating is part of that."

Merit just looked at the gumballs as they rolled down slides and through tunnels for a few moments. "You seem to feel pretty strongly about this for being a woman who won't date anyone seriously."

"I may not date anyone seriously, but I still date." Elise racked her brain, trying to figure out how to get this man to be willing to date. He was probably used to boardrooms and business plans and profit and loss sheets or whatever business owners did. And he was probably used to being very good at those things.

Maybe he just didn't like the idea of doing something he

knew he probably wouldn't be good at. He didn't want the embarrassment of crashing and burning.

"I've got it," she said. "Let's have a pretend date. You and me, right now. Then you can practice flirting, asking someone out, going on a date, all of it. Then next time will go better."

From the corner of her eye, Elise could see a smile spreading across his face. "Interesting plan."

"So do we have a deal?"

"Sure. Okay."

"Alright. Flirt with me."

"Hi," he said, leaning against the gumball machine, one arm still wrapped around his skateboard. "Come here often?"

Elise tried to hold back a laugh, but at the last second, it burst free. "Is this how you make business deals?"

A look of confusion flashed across his face, then he stood up straight.

"You're the CEO of a multi-million dollar company, right?"

He raised an eyebrow but nodded.

"Oh. North of multi-million." He lifted one shoulder in a minuscule shrug. "Oh—a good amount north of multi-million. Huh. Maybe I *should* Google you. Okay, so as the CEO of a *very* successful corporation, I'm sure you've sat in several meetings where you've tried to convince another very successful corporation to use your services, right? Or you've tried to negotiate with a supplier? What do you do there? It's basically the same thing. Just do what you know how to do."

He cleared his throat and set down the skateboard like it was the skateboard's fault that he wasn't acting like his normal, businesslike self. "Then we just chat. But first," he said, reaching down into his pocket and pulling out two quarters, "I'd like to buy the girl a gumball."

They left the candy store, and their chatting resumed, much as it had the rest of the afternoon. After they reached the end of the boardwalk, though, he stepped off of his skateboard.

"So," he said, stepping toward her as she stepped off hers, "I know that tradition dictates that I should ask you out for coffee sometime." He reached toward her arm, lightly placing his hand under her elbow, and Elise forced herself to ignore the thrill the touch gave her. "But I figured after a hot day in the sun, I would mix it up a bit. Would you like to get a soda with me sometime?" He nodded toward a soda shack a dozen feet away. "Like now, maybe?"

Everything about his voice was perfect, and his words seemed to roll right into her, caressing her as lightly as his touch on her arm. "Wow," she said. "Nice job on the ask out. How can I say no to that?"

After they got their sodas, they headed back toward the resort, riding their skateboards on the boardwalk and sipping their ice-cold drinks. When they reached the part of the boardwalk where they had originally entered, she said, "See? You're good at this Merit. Are you ready to date?"

"Not other people. But I did have a great time with you today. How about a second date?"

"What? No waiting until the day after, or at least a

couple of hours after to make contact again and ask me out?"

She hadn't planned on Merit going in this direction, so she stalled, trying to think things through. She was thrilled that Merit enjoyed their "date." But if she said yes to doing it again, would Graham consider it helping Merit get to where he needed to be? She wasn't just wanting the bonus, and she wasn't just wanting Graham to be happy. She wanted Merit himself to be happy. Would this help? Or would nudging him strongly toward meeting other guests at the resort be better?

She thought through what Graham's purpose in wanting Merit to go on dates must be. To give him experience in the dating world? So he could talk to women more easily? To get over any kind of fear of asking someone out? To become more comfortable with dating? Because if it was any of those reasons if he were "dating" her, it would accomplish that. She could help him with all of it, and he would be that much closer to experiencing all that Graham had hoped he would.

But if it was to find someone he could become more serious with, then dating her wouldn't do it.

"Okay, I've got this," Merit said. "You sit down right here. I'm going to go walk around that stage over there, and when I get back, we'll pretend that several hours have passed."

She smiled and nodded. Then when he hopped on his skateboard and started skating away, she pulled her phone out of her pocket and texted Graham.

> ELISE: Is your goal to have Merit date while he's here so that he can find someone to date long-term?

It only took a moment before Graham's response came through.

> GRAHAM: Goodness, no. There are plenty of women in Denver who he can date. He just needs to realize that he wants to date. Somewhere along the way he forgot that.

She pushed the phone back into her pocket. Being a stellar employee was high on Elise's list of important things, and helping Merit to meet the goals that Graham had set was what she had been asked to do for the four weeks he was at the resort. And one of those things was to get him to experience dating. It wasn't "real" dating and it was short-term, so the resort should be just fine with it.

When she felt the buzz from a text, Elise pulled out her phone. A text from Merit was on the screen.

> MERIT: I know it's only been a few hours since our last date, but I had such a great time. Would you like to go out again? Say yes, and I will let you pick the activity, and you won't get a single complaint from me.

Elise chuckled and looked up to see Merit leaning against the railing of the boardwalk only about ten feet away, skateboard resting with one end on the ground and the other in his hand. And instead of looking cheesy, like he had when leaning against the gumball machine, he was looking rather spectacular. His pose, and really, the man himself, was the most adorable mix of business and casual she had ever seen. That strong jaw, the confident air of someone used to making high-risk decisions, the relaxed broad shoulders, mixed with the crooked smile, the boyish charm, and the playful expression made him impossible to say no to.

Especially since he said he wouldn't complain at all about the activity. She smiled as she typed in her reply text.

> ELISE: A date would be lovely. I look forward to it, and since you are letting me pick the activity with zero complaints, I am thrilled to report that I have already signed us up for dance lessons every Tuesday, Thursday, and Saturday for the next two weeks, leading up to the Midsummer Ball.

She pressed *send*, then watched as he read the text, his face going through a myriad of emotions, all of which he tried to hide until he met her eyes again with a smile that showed all of his teeth and walked toward her. When he was only a couple of feet away, he said, "That sounds super exciting. I can't wait."

She laughed at how void of emotion the words came out. "I'm glad to hear you're so excited about it. I think this date is going to work out beautifully."

Nine

MERIT

MERIT PUT the lid on his water bottle and walked back onto the dance floor. It felt weird wearing gym pants, a t-shirt, and dress shoes, but Christian, the dance instructor, told them to wear the shoes to practice today that they'd be wearing at the ball on Saturday.

As strange as it felt, making the fashion faux pas he was sure he was making was worth it because Elise looked pretty adorable in her tennis skirt, tank top, and high heels that were nearly the same color as her skin.

"Everyone back to your places," Christian said. "Come on, back to your partners. All right, for most of you, this is your fifth lesson, and you've done well at the three dances we've practiced. Now that you're all warmed up with the steps of the cha cha, it's time to start adding your own flare to it."

Merit had never learned to dance and had always felt uncomfortable at dances, so when Elise had first said they were going to take lessons, he had serious regrets about texting that he wouldn't complain. He had gone to a handful of balls over the time that he'd been CEO of ZentCube, so he knew that it would be a useful skill to have, but he also knew how awful he had been at every one of those balls, and that made him want to run.

But for as much as he had been dreading the lessons, he'd ended up liking them quite a bit. And the biggest shock had been that he hadn't been terrible at it. He was no Christian Lopez and never would be, but he wasn't going to embarrass himself on Saturday night, and that was something.

Christian started the music and he and Shelly, the other dance instructor, danced the cha-cha in a much more complicated way. It was impressive and looked fun, but this was Merit's fifth lesson—there was no way he was going to be able to do half of that.

Elise leaned over. "We could do that part, don't you think?"

Both Christian and Shelly had been doing the normal footwork they had been practicing, with both of them facing each other, arms out, holding both hands, then they released one hand and pivoted outward, then back together. That was easy enough.

But then Shelly spun around several times, and then when she had her back to Christian, a good three feet apart, she leaned back into him. He caught her under her arms and walked backward, her heels dragging on the floor, but still, she was stepping one foot over the other as he pulled her. It looked cool, and her part seemed pretty difficult, but his part didn't seem too different from what they had been doing.

Merit tried to breathe out all the stress he was feeling that had nothing to do with dancing. "Let's try it and see."

Once Christian and Shelly stopped dancing and turned it over to them, Merit and Elise practiced, both counting the steps out loud. "Side, rock step, side together side, rock step, rock step, side together side. Cha cha cha, rock step, cha cha cha, rock step, side together side."

"Okay, now you lift my hand high."

Merit did, and Elise twirled around a few times, seeming to just know what she was supposed to do with her feet. She stopped with her back to him and then looked over her shoulder. "Ready to catch me?"

"Yep. I've got you."

She fell back into him, and he slid his hands under her arms. As he was walking backward, pulling her, she tried to do the step work but her legs got tangled, causing his legs to trip up, and they both nearly went down.

Laughing, Elise said, "Well, now we know that wasn't the way to do it. Let's try again."

He grasped her hand and pulled her to standing, not realizing that their feet had been so close together, which was now putting their faces so close together. And with those heels, she was only a couple of inches shorter than him. A blush rose to her cheeks, and she took a step back. If he had known that dance lessons would be full of moments like these, Elise never would've had to use a deal to get him to come—he'd have suggested it himself.

She kicked off her heels. "I think we should start without the handicap. When we get it, we'll try it with the heels."

He ended up pulling her, legs dragging but crossing over one another, in a full lap around the dance studio, half bare-footed and half with heels, stopping every few feet for her to do the backward fall into his arms until they finally decided that they got the step down. Then they tried the whole sequence together and nailed it, if he did say so himself. Both grinning, sweating, and panting from the fast-paced dancing, they kept dancing, adding new twists as they did.

Elise seemed to get comfortable with it all the quickest, and her hips were moving more and more as they danced, and she added in more arm motions as they danced, just doing whatever seemed natural. So he tried not to get too caught up in watching her and took her lead on adding flare.

As they danced, Christian came around, giving each couple advice and encouragement. As he got to them, Christian counted off to the beat they were dancing, "One two three cha-cha one two three. Looking good! Cha-cha-cha."

He reached out and pressed down on Merit's shoulders as their dancing brought them near him. "You're holding all your stress in your shoulders. Lower them a bit. Relax into it." Merit forced himself to release some of the stress he was feeling. "Good. You two are tearing it up on the dance floor over here! Nice job with the hip action and staying on the balls of your feet. Just last week you two kept looking down at your feet to see if you were doing it right, and you had those weak elbows and big steps, and look at you now! Bravo!"

Christian clapped three times loudly. "Let's take another break—grab some water, catch your breath, and then we'll slow things down a bit with a run-through of the Viennese Waltz."

"I'm glad I haven't missed any of my morning runs while I've been here," Merit said as they walked over to the wall. "I never knew dancing was so brutal."

Elise looked every bit as winded as he was. "So fun, though. I've suggested to so many guests that they take Christian's dance classes. I guess I should've been joining them."

She took a long drink of her water bottle, then closed the cap and studied him. "So how have things been going with getting separation from your company?"

"I talked to a few of my executives yesterday, but just as friends—I didn't try to pry for information even a little bit. And I've only tried hacking into Graham's email account twice this week."

Elise held a hand up and he gave it a high five. It seemed ridiculous to be high-fiving over something like cutting down on trying to get into your best friend's email account as a desperate bid for information, but it was a huge accomplishment. He was pretty proud of himself, and he liked that Elise was, too.

"And how about worrying about your company? It seems you're still carrying some of that stress around."

"I'm working on it." It turned out that had been one of

the more difficult parts to get past. He wasn't sure he was ever going to stop worrying about its success.

He was over halfway through his four weeks at The Royal Palm, and he had fallen into a nice rhythm. Mornings started with a workout and a run along the beach, then a mix of activities with Elise and meals and socializing with other guests, a phone call or texts from Graham most days, an introspective walk along the beach before bed, and thoughts of Elise running through his mind throughout.

Merit knew that Elise couldn't date guests, so he made sure not to make it look like they were dating whenever anyone was within sight. But even without any of that, he still loved doing all the activities with her.

She had taken their picture during a couple of their dates. The first was a game of racquetball, where they were in an enclosed room where no staff would see them getting a picture with their arms around each other, and the second was a ride on the Sky Wheel, the giant Ferris wheel on the boardwalk, where they got a picture at the very top, the ocean in the background, Elise planting a kiss on his cheek. She had texted him the pictures, and more than once, he'd pulled them up on his phone just to relive the moment a bit.

"So tell me," he said as they leaned against the wall of the dance studio, "what was the reason behind why you promised not to have a serious relationship until you were twenty-five? Because I've got to say, that's not one I've heard before. I'm guessing there's a story."

Christian clapped again and called everyone back to the dance floor, then started giving instructions, interrupting their conversation. "Normally, we do a dance showcase at the end of the lessons, but since your 'showcase' will be the Midsummer Ball, I want you all going in there confident on Saturday night. We're going to spend about ten minutes on each of the last two dances before we go, so you can keep them fresh in your mind." Shelly flipped the music on. "Starting with the Viennese Waltz. Show us what you've got."

Merit stood tall, his right hand high on Elise's back, his elbow raised high, her arm resting on his, his left hand outstretched to meet hers. Of the three dances they learned, this one was his favorite. The posture required for the dance made him feel like he could take on the world. It was a fast-moving yet graceful dance, and he got to hold Elise in his arms, their bodies nearly touching, as they danced, moving all the way around the dance floor.

"One two three, one two three," Christian called out. "Natural turn, one two three. Okay do a change step, then reverse turn, one two three. Excellent! Okay, keep going. You've got this."

Both Merit and Elise had caught on to this dance fairly quickly, and they moved as one across the dance floor. Never in his life had he guessed that dancing could make him feel so connected to a person.

"I believe you have a story for me," he said.

"I do," Elise said as they step, step, turned. "It's not super interesting, though. My mom got pregnant with me when she was eighteen—she found out two months before high school graduation."

"Change step, and reverse turn," Christian said over the sound of the music.

They switched the turn, still moving in the same direction around the outer edges of the dance studio.

"She and my dad were crazy in love, or at least they thought they were until she got pregnant. I guess at first it went well—they even got engaged."

"And now, ladies and gentlemen, let's see your fleckerl. Nice footwork on those spins! And your contra check. Beautiful!"

Christian was out on the dance floor, walking between the dancers. When he neared Merit and Elise, he reached out and gave a gentle push on Merit's shoulders. *No stress, no worries,* he told himself and lowered his shoulders into a more relaxed position.

As they transitioned back into the natural turn, he pushed, trying to get more from Elise. "I'm guessing they didn't get married?"

"Nope. Three weeks later, he decided he was too young and took off right after graduation. She only saw him once again, when he signed away his parental rights. So," she said as they did a change step to move into a reverse turn, "as you can imagine, my mom was a little wary of serious relationships too young. I promised her when I was sixteen that until I was twenty-five, I would only do group dates and casual dating. No serious relationships. On three, plant your feet. I want to try something. One two three."

Merit planted his feet, and instead of the normal footwork, she tightened her arms in his, then swung her legs up and out, one after another, both of them leaving the ground in an arc before landing back on the ground. It wasn't exactly graceful, especially since he hadn't known what she was about to do and so he hadn't supported her in the best way, but it looked fun.

"Let's try again," he said as they rounded one end of the dance studio. "One two three." This time, with both of them working together, it went better. It probably looked far from perfect, but it gave him a lightness in his chest stronger than he thought he could get, aside from having fantastic quarterly numbers to report.

"Your turn," she said.

"For what?"

"The move where you fling your legs out like I just did."

"Oh. Um."

"Come on. You've got an athletic build and you've proven yourself fairly nimble."

"Okay—it might work. You plant on three. One two three." Merit flung one leg out and up, pushing off with his other quickly after, momentarily transferring a good portion of his weight and balance to Elise as his legs arced out, but she didn't seem affected by it. And then his legs landed—not impressively gracefully as he had pictured—but he didn't fall, which for a split second had been a very real possibility.

Grinning and laughing, motions that felt completely at odds with the peaceful nature of the dance, they continued doing their natural turns around the outer ring of the dance floor.

The music shut off, and they stopped dancing, hands on

their hips, breathing heavily. "I think we may need to practice that a few more times to get it right."

Merit nodded. "Maybe somewhere with a soft landing."

As they walked over to their water bottles, Merit went back to the dating thing. A big part of the reason was that he wanted to know everything there was to know about this woman. But if he was being honest with himself, at least a part of the reason was that he wanted to know if dating her for real was even a remote possibility.

"So, you made a promise to your mom eight years ago. In all that time, you haven't tried to talk her into letting you off the hook on that promise? No one has come along who has made you want to bend the rule a bit?"

Elise had picked up her bottle, but stopped with her hand on the lid, not moving to open it. She just studied him, like she was trying to make a difficult decision. Then she looked down for a moment before meeting his eyes again and saying, "I can't exactly talk her into letting me off the hook. She died almost six years ago."

All the air whooshed out of Merit. He wanted to wrap his arms around Elise and hold her tight. He didn't know what it felt like to lose your only parent, but he had imagined exactly how it might feel enough times to guess.

Ten

THE LOOK on Merit's face was so full of care and concern that she wanted to reach out and press a hand to his cheek.

"How?"

"Cancer." She took a drink from her water bottle and then took a few more long breaths. "She was diagnosed in my senior year of high school. At about the same time of year that she had found out she was pregnant with me during her senior year, the doctors told me she had two months to live. Turns out it was a pretty accurate guess."

"That must have been so hard."

It was. And so was telling people about it. So much so that she had never told anyone she had dated before. The only people she had ever talked to about it outside of the people in Nestled Hollow who experienced it firsthand were Cyree, HallieMae, and her college roommates. But somehow in the past two weeks, she and Merit had gotten close enough that it felt more wrong not to tell him. "Well, it was just me and her my whole life. In many ways, she was my closest friend. So yeah, I miss her a lot. I've also had nearly six years to process it. I'm okay."

The look on his face told her that he felt terrible. Probably partly because he brought it up, although she never really understood why people felt bad about bringing up something they couldn't possibly have known anything about. But he probably also felt bad that she had lost her mom, and her only parent, so young. That was a look she had been used to getting from anyone that she told.

There was something more to his look, though. She gazed more deeply into his eyes, trying to figure it out. Then it hit her. That was the same look she gave people when she found out they had a parent pass away.

"You lost a parent, too."

Merit's eyebrows shot up and she worried that maybe she shouldn't have brought it up. But then he nodded. "My dad, when I was eleven. Massive heart attack. He was a real estate developer and was good at it—my family was pretty well off until then. But he had taken out a huge loan on our house when the market was high to fund some things and the market crashed and he lost big. I didn't understand a lot of it back then, but I could see that he was stressed to very unhealthy levels. A couple of months of not being able to find a way out, and he was gone."

Merit looked out across the dance floor, where the other couples were slowly making their way back into position to start the next dance. She reached out and placed a hand on his arm just to let him know she was there. Christian was walking toward his spot and Shelly toward the music.

"Do you want to leave?" Elise asked. "We don't have to stay for the last dance practice."

He scoffed. "And miss the foxtrot?"

She had deflected enough on her own to recognize that he wasn't wanting to keep thinking about his dad's death right now. Doing the foxtrot would certainly help, so they walked out onto the dance floor. "So, eleven," she said. "Isn't that the age when you started your first business?"

"Yep. My mom was left with a lot of debt and was working two jobs, and I wanted to help out." His chest puffed out a little. "I made fifty bucks that first summer."

She raised an eyebrow. "Impressive."

Shelly started the music, and she and Christian got set in the standard foxtrot position, which, from what Elise could tell, was pretty much the same as the Viennese Waltz position. "Now remember," Christian said as they demonstrated, "slow, slow, quick, quick. Slow, slow, quick, quick. Ready, go!"

Elise got into position with Merit, loving the way it felt to have his arm against her back, strong and secure, and to feel the muscles in his shoulder as she placed her arm on top of his. They started just doing the standard footwork, nothing fancy, Merit leading them around the floor.

"Oh, I get it," Elise said. "That's why you've been holding on to your business so tightly—you're afraid it will fail like your dad's did."

"What? No." He spun her out, still holding onto one

hand, then she spun back. "My business is nothing like my dad's."

"You're right. I'm glad that you understand that."

They moved around the floor, slow, slow, quick, quick, elbows high, other hands clasped outstretched.

"You said you weren't going to be my psychologist."

"Well, I did minor in psychology, so you'd be getting my services for free." He laughed, then she added, "But it doesn't take Psychology 101 to figure out that you've taken on the role of your dad and are afraid to fail at it."

He stepped out, both of them opening their arms, then coming back to touch, then releasing again.

"Nah. I just think that after watching my dad's business fail, I understand how easily it can happen."

They were getting comfortable enough with this dance that they were anticipating each other's moves pretty well. He shifted, steering them around another couple who was coming close.

"Okay, let's test that theory. You make a lot of money, right? Tell me what you spend it on."

"Well, a lot goes into money market accounts and retirement accounts and things like that. And of course living expenses, like utilities, food, gas, insurance."

"No—what do you *spend* it on?"

"College. I've got five younger brothers, and I wanted to make sure that all of them had the chance to go and live on campus. I have a brother who just graduated high school this year and will be starting at Stanford in the fall, and my youngest brother will be a high school senior. And rehab.

One of my brothers, Asher, has struggled with—well, a lot of things, including drug and alcohol addiction. And of course, I take care of my mom. She deserves it after she sacrificed so much for all of us."

She released his hand and spread hers wide like she was laying out the proof.

"Just because I've helped to take care of everyone in my family doesn't mean I've assumed the 'dad' role or that I'm afraid I'll make the same mistakes as him."

"Maybe not. There are a lot of aspects to the 'dad' role— not just earning money. But I don't think you need to worry so much about your company failing and losing everything. Sure, unexpected things happen, but if you did lose it all, it's not that big of a deal."

He laughed as they slow-slow-quick-quicked their way around the room. "I think you must not have any idea how much work went into building this company." He shook his head, seeming baffled at her suggestion.

"Merit," she said, stopping where they were. "You are obviously a very smart, very business-savvy guy. You're only twenty-six, and look what you've managed to build. Are you saying that if you lost everything, you wouldn't be able to start a new business and make it every bit as successful?"

He just blinked at her several times. Then he cocked his head to the side, like it wasn't something he'd thought about before, and said, "Huh."

After dance lessons, Elise headed to her offices. Yesterday, the day she normally spent on business stuff, Elise had played tennis with Merit, then she'd had to cover for Zabrena while she had an appointment, then she'd helped HallieMae with the game of Capture the Flag with the teens that spread across the pools, playground, and part of the beach, and then worked on last minute details for the Midsummer Ball with Kale. Which had left her with zero time to work on all the office duties. She was trying to be better about keeping up with that.

She attempted to work on schedules and emails and budgets, but she couldn't focus. All she seemed to be able to think about was Merit. Actually, he had been taking up more and more space in her thoughts for a while now. When she'd first met him, she had figured he was always going to be wrapped up in his own hard shell, with a focus that couldn't be torn from his business no matter what was going on around him.

But over the past fifteen days, she had witnessed a massive change in him—a change that was attracting her to him in so many ways she hadn't anticipated. She'd seen him be vulnerable several times, but never as much as he had while they'd been dancing. Or maybe she was feeling it extra because it was the first time she had also been vulnerable.

She had no idea how much money the guy was worth, but she suspected it was quite a bit. She also did not doubt that he drove a fancy car and lived in a house every bit as impressive as the one he was staying in at the resort. He hadn't mentioned those things when she asked what he spent his money on, though. His face had completely lit up when he had talked about helping his family, and that made her heart do crazy little flutters.

When she got a text from HallieMae saying *Come home and hang out with me. I'm sooooooo bored and my roommate is always gone*, she gave up getting more work done. She'd been thinking about Merit so much it wasn't like she was being productive anyway. She stopped by the staff cafeteria around the backside of the main lobby to grab a veggie pizza before heading back to their bungalow for the night.

"Oh my gosh, you brought food!" HallieMae said as soon as Elise stepped in the doorway. "I take back my negativity about you being gone all the time. You're the best roommate ever!"

Elise laughed. "HallieMae, we have food in the fridge."

"Yeah, but that food I have to make. It always tastes better when someone else makes it and brings it to you."

"So true." She pulled her phone out of her pocket when she felt the text. "No. No, no, no," she said, swiping the screen open so she could respond. "The people who are selling my childhood home just texted—they put an offer on a home and it was accepted, so they don't want to wait any longer to put my house on the market."

She quickly typed in *No, please don't yet! I'm supposed to get a bonus from work for the remainder that I need in 13 days. Please wait. PLEASE* and pressed send. Then she held her phone in both hands, staring at the screen, waiting to see the ellipses that showed they were typing a response.

Nothing. When the screen went dark, she touched it to bring it back to life.

They still weren't responding. She started to pace, still clutching the phone, staring at the screen. "What do I do? What if they aren't willing to wait? They said the housing market is booming there, so they may get an offer in twenty-four hours. Possibly even less."

"Well, the first thing you do," HallieMae said, pulling the phone out of her hands and setting it on the table, "is to not be a crazy-pants. Either they'll say they'll wait or they won't, and you stressing out won't change that."

"I know," she said, sitting down at the table.

HallieMae put a slice of pizza on a plate in front of her. "Eat."

Elise did as she was told and took a bite, then set the slice back on the plate. She chewed and swallowed without even noticing the taste. "But what if they say no? People don't move out of Nestled Hollow often. The fact that the house is back on the market after just six years is amazing—if someone else buys it, it could be fifty years before I get the chance again!"

"Then you can buy a different house in Nestled Hollow while you wait."

"It's not the same."

"I know. Your mom didn't live in a different house. I get it. Or at least I mostly do—I don't quite understand why you would leave this beach for a place where the annual snowfall has got your height beat by a few feet, but that's another thing. Elise, this house doesn't hold the key to your happiness."

"I know. You're right." Still, though, it did hold a huge amount of importance to her. It was home. And she hadn't had a home for far too long.

"I've got something that will distract you." HallieMae took a bite of pizza and said around her food, "Tell me about Merit."

Elise's eyes jerked to HallieMae's. "Why?" Did she suspect something was going on between the two of them? Whether she was asking because she saw one of their dates or guessed the very real attraction she was feeling toward him, both were bad.

HallieMae shrugged and took another bite, acting like it was just a conversation topic, nothing more. "He's cute, and you've spent a lot of time with him. What's he like?"

"Well, I thought he was a money-hungry jerk who didn't know how to have fun. It turns out that he isn't as money-hungry as I thought, and once upon a time, he *did* know how to have fun. I think he's finding that version of himself again."

"Nice! Good work. Have you found out what kind of car he drives yet?"

Elise chuckled, shaking her head and taking a bite of pizza.

"Zabrena said he took his shirt off at Sand Castle Creations and that it was a pretty earth-shaking moment. I'm jealous you didn't invite me."

"Hal!"

"I know, I know. No ogling the guests. If that's an official rule, by the way, you should probably let Zabrena know. Because I'm going to tell you right now that she was totally ogling."

Elise's phone buzzed, and she nearly knocked it off the table in her rush to grab it. The screen lit up to show a text that read *Okay, we'll wait 13 days. But if you're not ready by then, I'm sorry—we'll have to list it.*

She exhaled all the stress she had been holding in and typed back, *Thank you! I'll be ready.*

Elise chatted with HallieMae for a while, and then her roommate started getting texts from the guy who worked at the Mini Palm that she had a crush on, and retreated to her bedroom. So Elise walked out on her balcony to enjoy the sunset.

Or maybe she went out on the patio to enjoy Merit. She had seen him walking along the beach, deep in thought, a couple of times before, and just like she had hoped, she spotted him out there today, too. A really big part of her wanted to head down there and join him. To walk with him, talk with him, ask him what he was thinking about, and enjoy his company.

She forced that part of her back, even though it took all her willpower. They already spent so much time together that she was having a very hard time not falling for him more fully than she had ever fallen for someone before. Meeting him at additional, unplanned times would only make that worse.

She wasn't twenty-five yet, and that promise to her mom

was as good as set in stone. So were the rules at The Royal Palm. The timing wasn't right for him, either. Right now he had plenty of time to spend with someone. But the moment he went back home, things would get busy for him again just like they had been before, and he would no longer have time to go do fun activities or take relaxing walks along the beach. So, getting her heart more involved was a very bad idea.

Eleven

MERIT

MERIT MET Elise at the fountain in the center court of the resort at nine the next morning, just like she'd requested. She still hadn't told him what they were doing, so he looked around as he waited, hoping to see some kind of clue. Something at the beach? The pool? Something outside of the resort? Art lessons? With her, he had learned to expect anything.

She rushed up the pathway from the direction of the activities building. "Good morning! I'm so sorry I'm late. There have been a lot of last-minute details to work out for the ball tomorrow. Are you ready for today?"

He fell into step beside her as she led them along the shrub-lined pathway. "I honestly have no idea if I am."

Elise laughed. "There's not a lot you need to be prepared for today. It's a sit back and relax day."

"You're going to make me go to a movie finally, aren't you?"

She grinned. "Something even better." They rounded a corner, and she motioned to a building that said *Royal Touch* above the doors in a minimalistic yet stylish font.

He couldn't put his finger on exactly why, but he was suddenly nervous. Someone dressed in white opened the glass door and welcomed them inside. They walked into a large lobby with glass curving ceilings arcing high above them. White couches, white fluffy rugs, and white curtains filled the space, with white walls and white columns rising to where the ceiling lowered to lead to the back part of the building, all in that same minimalistic yet fashionable style.

"Welcome to Royal Touch," the woman said. "My name is Dixie, and we're going to take good care of you today."

"What does she mean, 'take good care of us?'" Merit asked, feeling wary enough that he was having a hard time keeping his feet planted where they were and not heading back out the door at a run.

"I was noticing while we were dancing that you're still holding a lot of stress, so I wanted you to do something that would help you to relax. This is the day spa, and I have a massage, body scrub, and mud treatment lined up."

Okay, now he really was going to bolt. If Elise wanted him to have a relaxing day, this was not it.

"Don't look so terrified!" Elise said. "Dixie here is wonderful. She's got a great staff, and you are going to leave here feeling pretty heavenly."

His eyes flew to hers, the hairs on his arms lifting. "You aren't going to do it with me?" His shoulders felt even tighter than they had been a few minutes ago.

"No, but don't worry. You'll only be alone here when you're changing."

"You can't leave me here."

She sighed. "Merit, I can't stay."

"Why not?"

"Because..." Her ears were turning red and she shuffled her feet, trying not to look down. Then she huffed. "Because even with my discount, I can't exactly afford this place, so I didn't book a session for me."

"But I can." The urgency in his voice was coming out loud and clear, but he didn't care. He stepped closer to Dixie. "Do you have space for Elise to join me?"

"We did have a cancellation for a couples spa day today, and as a VIP guest, you do get a first chance at the appointment."

He turned to Elise. "Do you have commitments today you can't get out of? Please tell me no. Please join me." Why did he ever think it was a good idea to say that he wouldn't say no to any activity she planned? If there was an actual phobia of spas, he was pretty sure he had it. The place made him think of hospitals, and just like hospitals, once you went through the doors leading past the lobby, there were scary, unknown tests.

"I, no, but—" She turned to Dixie like she was going to get her out of it or something. Then she turned back to him. "I just..." He studied her, trying to figure out why she was suddenly so flustered.

"Do you not want to?" Her unwillingness only made him more nervous. He didn't know why she would've suggested he come to the spa if it wasn't something she was willing to do herself.

"No, I *do*," Elise said. "I would kill for a spa day. It's just —" She turned back to Dixie. "We're not exactly a couple. We're not even dating. I mean, obviously, since he's a guest and I work here. I just don't think..."

At first, he didn't have a clue what her ramblings were about. Then it slowly started dawning on him, and a smile began to form on his face.

"Honey," Dixie said, reaching out and placing her hand on Elise's forearm, "no one has to be naked under the sheets if they don't want to be. We have bathing suits here for both of you to use. And although you'll be in the same room for the mud treatment, you'll be on different beds, so no need to worry about anything."

The woman led them through the doors and into the back part of the building, and Merit's heart rate doubled and his palms got sweaty. He didn't know why. Objectively, the place was beautiful and clean and peaceful, and relaxing music played quietly through speakers he couldn't even see.

She stopped at some cupboards in a big open area with some more couches and pulled out some black items that he guessed were the swimsuits. Then she led them down a different hallway and opened double doors leading into a room and held out her hand, directing them to go inside.

Elise walked in first, and Merit entered right after her. The room was open and spacious and had two massage beds in the middle, separated from each other by a good five feet. Dixie handed them the black items.

"There's two bathrooms. Yours is over there, Elise, and yours, Merit, is on that side. Go ahead and get changed into your suits, and then you can come out and get on the beds. There's a sheet right here on top to cover yourselves with. Rachel and Nadia will be in to get started in about five minutes."

Merit changed in his bathroom, which also had a shower and shelves to put his things on. The suit, though, was shorts that would've been short in the eighties and were a little too snug for his liking. He got back out into the main room more quickly than Elise. He thought about getting under the sheet so he wasn't just standing there in tight shorts when she came out, but somehow that felt every bit as awkward. So he pulled the sheet off the bed and tied it on over one shoulder like a toga.

He walked over and checked out a water feature that ran down one wall of the room, over differently colored glass stones. A water feature had come with his house back in Denver, but he never really understood why someone would want something that constantly made them think they left the water on somewhere.

When he heard Elise's door open, he turned to face her and made his best imitation of a Greek statue. Elise laughed out loud—a big, hearty, appreciative laugh that made him feel lighter. Not that it made him feel less creeped out by the place.

Elise's swimsuit wasn't too different from his—short, snug shorts, with a short tank top that showed her stomach. She appeared about as comfortable in it as he was in his, but she seemed to like his toga idea. So she pulled hers off the other bed with a flourish and tied it around her like a toga, too.

"Thanks for staying with me. This place..." He didn't know how to finish his sentence. "Makes me uncomfortable" didn't seem like a very manly thing to say.

"You're welcome. But Merit, I was so concerned about the suits in the lobby that I skipped right past the price. She gave me the total when I booked your visit, so I know how expensive it is and, well, let's just say that it's enough to buy a car that would probably get you to work every day without breaking down."

Merit brushed off the total. "Whatever amount it is, it's worth it."

"Does this place freak you out that much?"

"Everything that goes on back here is a mystery. I read a spa 'menu' once when one of my executives was trying to get me to go, and I had no clue what any of the items even were." He looked around the sparse, clean, supposedly relaxing room. "Plus, it just feels unnaturally peaceful here."

"Really?" she said, looking around at the same things he was looking at. "I think it's nice. I wouldn't want to work here or anything—I need a little more adventure in my life—but I don't know. I kind of like it."

"It feels wrong."

She stopped and studied him, tilting her head to the side. After a moment's consideration, she said, "I'm just wondering. Maybe you've been in a constant state of stress for so long that this calm peacefulness is simply at odds with your inner," she fluttered her hands over her head and torso like she was trying to find a word that referred to what was on the inside, "self."

His brow crinkled as he thought about that.

"You know, like how some people enjoy loud, chaotic music because what they've got going on in their head is loud and chaotic, so it feels at home. But if someone else whose head is calmer and more relaxed listens to the loud and chaotic music, it feels at odds with what's going on in their head, so they try to get away from it as quickly as possible."

Merit nodded. Maybe that was it.

The doors opened, and two women walked in who were probably just younger than he and Elise were, one of them pushing a cart with supplies and towels. The brown-haired one raised an eyebrow ever so slightly at their togas, and Merit knew that if there was some spa technician *Crazy Things I've Seen at Work* list, they were going on it. The woman said, "Hello, I'm Rachel and this is Nadia. Do you have any questions before we get started?"

Her voice came out calm and relaxing like she was a deejay on a radio station that only played elevator music. At first, Merit was annoyed, like nails on a chalkboard, but then he thought of Elise's theory and just tried to get himself to relax.

Elise glanced at Merit, actually looking as nervous as he was, then said, "We're both first-timers. So if you don't mind talking us through everything as you go, we would appreciate it."

Apparently, Merit had been holding his breath, because that made him start breathing again.

"Okay," Nadia said, "we'll just need you both to lie down, and we'll cover you with the sheet. Then we'll only uncover the part we're working on, so you'll never be fully uncovered."

They both got on the beds and the technicians covered them up. He glanced over at Elise, and she gave him a big smile and two thumbs up. It made him smile.

Rachel grabbed a plastic bottle off the cart. "First we start by rubbing hot grapeseed oil on your skin, and we give you a bit of a massage as we do it. It's high in antioxidants and makes your skin feel amazing. Then we'll put on the dead sea salt scrub. It'll feel pretty gritty as we do it, but that exfoliates all the dead skin, too."

"And it'll feel like the most amazing back scratch ever," Nadia said. "It increases blood flow, too, and gives your skin lots of nutrients."

"We'll start with your backs, then we'll wipe off the salt and oil with a steamed towel before we have you turn over to your front, then we'll do the same to your legs. Good?"

That didn't sound so bad. He had normal massages now and then when his shoulders and neck muscles got particularly tense, and this sounded pretty similar. He glanced over at Elise. She looked like she was okay with it, too, so he rolled over onto his stomach and positioned his face in the head support so he could breathe.

The technician started rubbing his back with the hot oil and it felt great. Phenomenally great, even. It was like she was rubbing every bit of stress out of his shoulders and back, while he just sunk into the table.

"Oh, wow," Elise said, muffled through the table, "that salt really does feel amazing."

Merit almost turned his head to look in her direction, but then just said through the hole in the table, "You're already on to the salt part?"

"It's not a race," Rachel said. "You're going to take a little longer because you're holding a lot of stress in your shoulders."

Merit cleared his throat. "Yeah, I've been told that."

He heard Elise chuckle.

"You two are supposed to be relaxing," Nadia said. "Try thinking of things that make you happy. It'll help you fully relax so all of this can work better."

Ten minutes later, when Rachel was wiping the last of the salt and oil off his legs, Merit was surprised to realize that his "happy thoughts" had been spread pretty equally between his company and Elise. His mind had gone through all of the time he had spent with Elise over the past two weeks, how much he had been enjoying who he was when he was around her, and about all the little things he liked about her. Every time she shared more about herself, he realized more and more how amazing she was and how much he wanted to know more.

He had also been thinking of new ideas for his company. After his first couple of days here, the ideas had been coming daily. New and different ideas that he hadn't even begun to consider yet. Ideas that were going to help his company and employees grow and become stronger, better, and more creative.

Merit looked over to where Elise lay on her back on the massage table, the sheet covering up to her shoulders, her face looking relaxed and blissful and so beautiful. He had always thought that he could either have his company or a relationship and that trying to have both would mean that one would fail miserably.

But maybe he had been wrong. Maybe there was a way to have both.

Twelve

ELISE

Elise lay on the massage table, her body like Jell-O, feeling blissful in every cell of her body. She didn't need much in life —her focus on paying off student debt and saving to buy back her house was fierce. She had learned to live off next to nothing just so she could funnel as much as possible into those goals.

But man. When she met those goals, she'd have to start a fund to save for another massage like this. Every bit of her felt incredible.

Rachel and Nadia started stirring tubs of a greenish-brown substance that had been sitting on some kind of warmer. Then they explained how they were going to paint mud on their bodies.

"You're going to…" Merit rose on his elbows and looked skeptically back and forth between Nadia and Rachel, then to Elise. "*Paint* mud onto us?"

"You trusted me with the salt and oil," Rachel said. "How was that?"

"Weird, but it felt great."

"Then trust me with the mud."

He looked at Elise, and she gave him an enthusiastic smile and two thumbs up, so he said, "All right then. Mud it is."

Nadia had her sit up first so she could start by painting her back. The mud was warm and soft and smooth and really just made her back feel wet. Then she lay down and Nadia painted the rest of her.

"This mud is from the Dead Sea," Nadia said as she worked. "It's some of the most incredible stuff on earth. This isn't only going to feel good while you're here. Between all the antioxidants your skin is taking in and all the toxins this mud will pull out, you'll both be feeling great for a very long time after."

"Now we just need to cocoon you," Rachel said.

Merit raised his head. "Cocoon?"

"Just keep trusting me," Rachel told him.

It didn't take long to figure out what Nadia meant. With Elise's arms at her sides, Nadia wrapped the bottom sheet around her, then wrapped the thin sheet of plastic that was under that, then put a thermal blanket on top of her, tucking it in the sides, then a thick blanket, then a steamed towel.

With each layer, she got a little more claustrophobic. Her arms were trapped in there pretty tightly! If she panicked and needed one of them out, or if she just needed to scratch her nose—which was feeling itchy just thinking about it—then she couldn't.

As she felt the panic rising, she moved her arm around a bit. Okay, she could probably get it out on her own. It would mess up all of Nadia's careful tucking and probably would mess up the mud, too, but it was possible. She just needed to know it was possible. She tried to relax and just enjoy the heat. It reminded her of laying on the beach in the warm summer sun. *Just focus on the heat*, she told herself.

"Is it supposed to be this hot?" Merit asked.

Rachel nodded. "It helps to bring out the toxins. We'll let you two just relax for about twenty minutes, then we'll be back in to unwrap you and clean off the mud."

As soon as the two girls left, Merit said, "I don't think I can last that long in this heat."

"That's your Colorado blood talking." She twisted so she could see him. "If this were ten degrees instead of one hundred, you'd probably be just fine."

He laughed. "True. You doing okay over there?"

"As long as I don't think about my arms being trapped, yes."

"Ahh. A claustrophobic."

"I didn't think I was until now. Are you really fine being trapped?"

"Yep."

"Then talk to me. Distract me. What have you thought of this so far?"

He met her eyes for a few moments, just looking at her. "I was wondering if this might help my mom."

"Oh yeah? In what way? Did you get the 'holding stress in your shoulders' gene from her?"

He chuckled. "No, actually I was wondering if it might keep her healthy. She had cancer, too—Chronic Myelogenous Leukemia."

"Oh, I am so sorry." She searched his face, suddenly understanding what his expression meant when she told him that her mom had died. It was likely a possibility for him once, too. "I'm sorry. How is she doing?"

"The odds were against her, but she's been cancer free for three years." His smile made his ears move. "I just don't want her to relapse, because that's always so much worse. Each year that goes by without a relapse is a gift. I just want to do all I can to keep making sure she gets those years."

Elise hated being in this cocoon right now. She wanted to put her arms around him and hold him tight and tell him that she understood what he went through and that he could unload any of the weight he'd been carrying about it onto her shoulders.

But she was trapped.

"Maybe getting rid of toxins would help her stay cancer free." He glanced down at his own cocoon. "As I'm laying here, sweating it out in this furnace, imagining all the toxins leaving my body, I keep thinking of her being here." He chuckled. "She'd enjoy it more—she's always cold. This would probably be heaven to her."

"You should bring her. Or find a place that does this in Colorado."

"I should."

"Merit?"

"Yeah?"

"This isn't something you talk about often, is it?"

He shook his head.

"Thank you for sharing it with me. I know it can be lonely to have your only parent get a possibly terminal illness and feel like no one quite understands what it was like to have lived through it. Know that you can talk to me about it anytime."

Merit looked into her eyes, and she felt like he was seeing right inside her. That there was a connection between them that reached somewhere deeper than any other relationship she had experienced with anyone. He gave her a nod as the doors opened and Rachel and Nadia walked in.

They unwrapped her and Merit, and Elise put her arms straight out and waved them around, just because she could. After they wiped all the mud off with steamed towels, they had them each go into their own restrooms and shower to get any remnants off. Once they were back in the room with the beds, clean and wrapped in fluffy bathrobes, they led them down the hall and into a room with their private cabana.

Plates of fruit sat on a table next to a window overlooking the beach, and stairs led up to a square pool of water that looked like it was at least 8 feet long and wide.

"These mineral waters have healing powers," Rachel said. "And now that you're free of dry skin and anything else that would impede its ability to take in nutrients, these waters will have an even greater effect. So feel free to eat the fruit and hop into the warm waters to soak and enjoy. We'll be back to get you in about an hour."

"Pool or fruit—I don't know which is pulling me more," Elise said. "Oh wow! Check out the size of these raspberries!"

Merit made his way up to the pool, but Elise couldn't walk away from the blueberries and blackberries and strawberries and raspberries. She tried one of each, each one bursting on her tongue with flavor and freshness and sweetness. She closed her eyes as she savored each one.

Of course, the man floating in the pool was pulling her in that direction pretty well, too. If there was ever someone who taught her that she shouldn't judge a person based on the little a first impression showed, it was Merit. She ignored the rest of the berries and climbed the steps to the pool.

"Oh," she said as she stepped down into the water. "It feels…"

"Heavier."

She nodded and lowered herself the rest of the way into the pool, sitting on one of the seats at the side, her shoulders submerged. The water was just warm enough to feel comfortable, without being so hot that they would have to get out soon.

"So," Merit said, his arms swooshing back and forth in the water, "tell me. How does a small-town girl from the mountains of Colorado find herself working at the nicest resort in Myrtle Beach?"

It was also an extremely personal question that she didn't share the answer to often, but she found herself wanting to tell him. "My mom never married, and so, as a single mom, she had to work a lot. You know how it is. Anyway, working and raising a daughter just became her entire life. So when she was first diagnosed with cancer—back before we knew it was terminal—she started thinking about all the things she never did that she wanted to do and always figured she'd have time for later.

"So we sat down and made a bucket list. While most kids in my grade were writing essays for college scholarships and going on ski weekends and taking off to warmer climates for spring break, my mom and I were doing all those things on her bucket list."

She smiled remembering those last days with her mom. It had been hard, worrying about what the cancer might do, and then finding out what exactly it would do. But it had also been a time when she and her mom had focused nearly all their attention on each other, and she was so glad she got the chance to get closer to her during those months.

"We got to a lot of them. We did so many fun things together, and it was great to see my mom finally getting to do the things she had been waiting her whole life to do." She shook her head. "But we couldn't get to all of them. She just got too sick, and the cancer treatments made her even weaker."

She looked up at the ceiling, trying to keep her emotions in check. He hadn't asked her to tell him about her mom's death; he had asked her to tell him about her career choice. She cleared her throat. "We had her funeral three days before graduation. I came home after the ceremony, still wearing my cap and gown, and I picked up the bucket list from the kitchen counter. It was just so sad that she had so many dreams that she didn't get to fulfill, you know?

"So I decided right then that I wanted a job where I could help people do their bucket list items. To help them to enjoy all that life has to offer while they're living it, not just when they're in the process of dying from it.

"The biggest thing on her list that we never got to was seeing the ocean and hanging out on a beach. On the days when she was too sick to get out of bed, she researched exactly where she wanted to go to see the ocean, and she picked here. Not just South Carolina or Myrtle Beach, but The Royal Palm specifically. It was dreaming of this place that got her through the worst times.

"So I found out everything I could about the place, decided what job I wanted, then went to college to get the degree that would best put me in the position to get it. I've been here three years now, doing exactly what I had hoped to do."

"I bet your mom would be happy, knowing that you chose what you were going to do, and then went for it like that."

"I hope so. And I hope she's proud of what I'm doing since it's something she knows is important."

"Now I understand why you were so annoyed with me when I first got here. I wasn't enjoying all life has to offer."

"I wasn't annoyed."

"You were a little bit."

"Okay, I was. So," she said, "now that you've gotten

through most of the scary parts, what do you think of today?"

"I think this is the most relaxed I've been since I was ten."

A smile spread across her face. She hoped Merit would leave here still determined to live life. Seeing his transformation was exactly the kind of thing she had hoped she would get to take part in back when she was freshly graduated, figuring out what she wanted to do with her life.

"This water is amazing." He held his arm out. "And check out how soft my skin is." He seemed to suddenly realize that they were hanging out in nothing but swimsuits and that he asked her to touch him and pulled his arm back a little. But it was too late. She reached forward and ran her fingers down the muscle of his upper arm.

"Wow!" She ran her fingers down it again, then she touched her own arm—it was just as soft. She held it toward Merit. "Check out mine."

He touched her arm and suddenly the feel of the room changed. They both backed away, hesitant.

Merit cleared his throat and changed the subject. "If you've been here for three years, then you graduated from college early."

She moved her arms around in the water. "I spent that first summer packing up all our stuff and dealing with paperwork and putting the house up for sale and all that kind of stuff. Then I moved to a college dorm. I no longer had a home to go to, so I just went to school right through the summer semesters and lived on campus from my first day of college to my last. It meant I had a lot of student loans, which wasn't fun, but," she drew out the word, "I'm happy to report that they are all paid off!"

She was pretty proud of herself for that. It had taken a lot of focus and sacrifice, but she'd managed to pay them off in the same amount of time that it had taken to rack them up. Merit looked pretty impressed, too, which made her smile even bigger.

"Now, though, I'm saving up to buy back my childhood home. That excites me even more than paying off student debt, so I've been focusing on saving pretty fiercely."

"Your home in Nestled Hollow?" He looked surprised and confused. "From everything I had gathered about you, I thought you were loving it here."

"I *do*. I love it a lot. I love what I do here. And at the very least, I'll be here every year for the busy season, which is four months a year or sometimes more, for as long as they'll have me. But," she said, feeling bold and daring, revealing so much about herself, "for six years, my 'permanent' address has been a college dorm and a vacation resort. I need a *home*."

He looked so intensely in her eyes—so much depth of emotion on his face that she couldn't interpret it all. But he seemed to get it on a level that no one else ever had. The connection between them felt so strong that she could no longer have it just be an emotional connection. She needed to touch him. She reached out and ran her fingertips from his temple to his jaw. He leaned into her hand, resting his jaw on her knuckles.

Then he reached out and put his finger under her chin, his thumb grazing her lips. She moved closer in the water toward him, her eyes focused on his. She glanced at his lips and wanted this connection they were feeling to be even stronger. She wanted to feel those lips on hers. Moving her hand around to the back of his head, she ran her fingers through his wet hair, pulling herself ever so slowly closer to him. As she kept her eyes on those beautiful green ones of his, she could tell that he wanted this every bit as much as she did.

Elise heard a sound from the door a split second before Nadia opened it, calling out, "What do you think of the mineral waters?"

Elise and Merit separated quickly—fast enough that she was pretty sure that neither Nadia nor Rachel saw them about to kiss. She could still feel the shock, surprise, guilt, and lingering yearning for Merit on her face, so she tried to relax it into a calm, peaceful expression.

"It was wonderful," Merit said as he climbed the stairs out of the pool, and she could tell that he was talking about more than just the water.

"Isn't it?" Rachel said. "I love it. Go ahead and put on your bathrobes, and we'll lead you to your pedicures."

Merit looked back at her, and instead of having terror on his face like she'd have guessed earlier at the thought of pedicures, the only look on his face told her he really wished their kiss hadn't been interrupted.

Thirteen

MERIT

MERIT HAD KNOWN that Elise was going to be busy doing all the last-minute preparations for the Midsummer Ball from the time they had left the day spa yesterday until it was time to be seated for the dinner today. So after his morning run and exercises, he had left to explore the city of Myrtle Beach outside of the resort and didn't return until it was time to start getting ready for the dance.

The moment he'd used his key card to open the front door of the mansion, though, something felt off.

"Hello?" he called out as he closed the door.

He waited a moment in the high-ceilinged entryway, looking toward the railing to the floor above and glancing at the rooms and hallways he could see from where he stood, then walked back toward the great room. As soon as he stepped from the hallway to the room, two people jumped out and yelled, "Surprise!"

"Graham! Tessa! What are you doing here?" He tried to

calm his pounding heart as Tessa gave him a welcome hug and Graham clapped him on the back.

"We wanted to surprise you and see how you were doing," Tessa said.

"You certainly surprised me."

"Come in, come in," Graham said like he was welcoming him into his place instead of showing up at Merit's. Except Graham was the one who booked everything, so it was probably on the resort's record as Graham's place. "I've been getting Elise's nightly reports, but I want to see how you are doing with my own eyes."

"I'm good. How long are you staying?"

"Just until tomorrow afternoon."

"We wanted to make sure we were here for the ball," Tessa added. "Graham has been showing me the pictures Elise has been sending of the two of you, and I think you are just adorable together. I can't wait to meet her tonight."

"You have tickets to the ball?" He rubbed the back of his neck and tried to ignore the weight in the pit of his stomach.

"Of course!" Graham said. "I bought them and our plane tickets the same day I booked this place."

The two of them were leading him to the couches, but he said, "I've been out all day. Let me just run to the restroom, then I'll be right in."

He calmly walked down the hallway to the bathroom and shut the door, then pulled out his phone and started typing.

MERIT: GRAHAM IS HERE AT THE RESORT. His wife, Tessa, too. I thought I was doing good, but now he'll be able to see in person how I'm doing. What if he doesn't think I've been doing enough?

They have tickets to the ball and can't wait to see the two of us together. But I know we can't act like we very nearly kissed yesterday around any Royal Palm staff.

He paced as much as he could in the small room, waiting for her response. Finally, his phone buzzed and he looked down at it.

ELISE: Merit, they are going to be blown away at the difference they'll see in you. You don't need to worry one bit.

My staff and all the rest of the employees working the event know that I'm working with you, so it won't be weird that we're together the whole time. They know we've done dancing lessons, too, so that won't be suspicious. If our performance makes anyone at The Royal Palm question anything, we'll just tell them it was all part of the dance.

No worries.

We've got this.

He typed back, *I hope so. See you soon*, and then put his phone back in his pocket.

He didn't know if this bathroom was too far away from

the great room to be heard, but just in case, he flushed the toilet and washed his hands, then headed back to talk to Graham and Tessa.

Merit, Graham, and Tessa made their way to the line of people who were waiting to be checked in to the Midsummer Ball, just down the pathway to the restaurant area they had set up on wooden flooring on the beach. Never had he been so nervous getting ready for something before. Not even high school prom.

Of course, when he was getting ready for his high school prom, he hadn't had the added obstacle of that almost-kiss with Elise running through his mind.

And now he could see her, dressed in a stunning sky blue dress and those heels that were almost the same color as her skin that she'd worn to their last practice, her hair pulled up in curls, checking on all the last-minute items. She was moving from one end of the restaurant area to the other end of the dance flooring to the platform where the band's equipment was set up, so she didn't even notice that they were in line until they were checking in.

As soon as Elise's eyes found him, she rushed over to greet them. She gave Merit a smile that melted him a little and looked like she maybe wanted to greet him with more than a smile. He wished she could, too. Then Graham took her hand in both of his, where he half shook it and half cradled it, thanking her warmly for her time with Merit.

Then Tessa shook her hand and thanked her much the same way.

"And I hear that congratulations are in order," Elise said.

Graham smiled and put a hand on Tessa's stomach, which was barely showing a bump in the dress she was wearing. "Thank you. We're pretty excited for this little kiddo to join us."

As they were walking to their table, Elise turned to him and mouthed, "They're nice."

He chuckled and nodded. A little too eager to be helpful sometimes, but nice.

Merit pulled the chair out for Elise and tucked it in as she sat, and then took the seat next to her.

Elise pulled her phone out of her purse and laid it on the table. "I apologize for having my phone out. I am the lead on this event, and I'll likely have to continue putting out some fires as we eat."

"That's no problem at all," Tessa said.

The four of them chatted and Elise was gracious and amazing and he couldn't help listening to her with a smile spread across his face. Maybe he was glad that Graham showed up because now when Merit talked about her, he would know how great she was.

He relaxed as they waited for the last of the people to get checked in and seated, and after all the time they'd spent together and especially after yesterday, he leaned back in his chair and without thinking about it, draped his arm over the back of her chair.

Elise stiffened and her eyes darted to the side, as if she

wanted to look all around to see if anyone was looking, but stopped herself. He pulled his arm back. He'd gotten so caught up in the conversation that he'd completely forgotten that all of her staff was here, along with a couple of dozen other employees of The Royal Palm, including her two bosses.

Before long, the wait staff started bringing around plates of salad and placing one in front of each of them. Elise was looking around at all the different areas, and Merit was sure she was checking to make sure everything was going well. He could practically feel Graham and Tessa questioning Elise's behavior and suddenly he saw it through their eyes. He realized that to them, it probably looked like Elise wasn't interested in their company and was looking to be anywhere but there.

She must've realized it, too, because she said, "I feel so guilty sitting here, eating and having an enjoyable time while my staff is taking care of everything. Usually, I'm out there with them."

"Don't you worry about us," Graham said. "We understand. Take care of whatever you need to take care of."

Elise smiled at Graham and Tessa, then turned to Merit. "Did you have fun out exploring Myrtle Beach today?" She had laid her hand on his leg when she asked, then quickly pulled it back. It was a good thing she remembered as quickly as she did because HallieMae came up to her other side just a few seconds later and handed her a small piece of paper.

"These are the guests who haven't checked in yet. The

hostess would like to know if those spots can be given to people on the waitlist."

Elise scanned the list, then said, "Only these two spots. The other guests will be here."

After HallieMae left, Elise picked up her phone, looked at the screen, and then sighed. "I am so sorry. There's a problem with one of the amps for the band, and I need to get our backup one from the activities building storeroom."

Everyone's eyes went to the platform where the band would be performing, where two people were fiddling with some equipment.

"Merit—it's kind of high. Do you mind helping me?"

"Not at all." He dabbed at his mouth with his napkin, then set it on the table and followed her away from the restaurant area. He was secretly hoping that when they got back into the storeroom, they might have a moment close together in the cramped quarters where that missed kiss opportunity might present itself again.

Elise strode forward and he had to walk fast to keep up. As soon as they were around the corner of a building and hidden from view of the ball, she stopped. "Merit, I can't do this! I can't pull off a convincing job of faking."

Oh.

So no chance of that kiss after all. Merit looked down. She had probably just been trying to show Graham that she was doing the job that he had hired her to do, and maybe she didn't think that he was to the point Graham wanted him to be, so she felt like she had to fake it. Knowing Graham, he had probably offered her a bonus if she helped him to meet all four stipulations. He looked up and met her eyes. "Listen, it's okay. You don't need to fake it. If Graham doesn't think I've progressed enough—"

Elise swatted at him with the back of her hand. "I'm not having trouble faking that you're doing well." She rolled her eyes. "My problem is I can't fake that nothing is going on between us with my staff. They know me too well, and I am pretty sure that every single action or word or facial expression is tipping them off that I have feelings for you."

"You have feelings for me."

"Yes! Obviously. Merit, I don't know what to do. I have given my staff so much grief about not dating guests that I can't finish out this dinner and dancing, blatantly going against those rules."

He put his hands on her shoulders and tried not to smile too much that this was her big problem.

"Merit, I'm not the kind of person who does that."

He let out a long breath, thinking. "How about this: we both go back there and we direct all our conversation to Graham and Tessa. We ask them questions and answer by looking only at them. We don't look at each other at all, so nothing can tip anyone off. And then we'll just, I don't know, try to stay apart while I'm a guest here."

She nodded. "Okay, that might work."

"There isn't a problem with the amp, is there?"

"Nope."

They started walking back to the dining area, and Merit suddenly realized that he couldn't even walk next to her without feeling like he was putting off vibes that he liked her. No wonder she was worried about her staff noticing.

"Did you get it all worked out?" Graham asked as they sat back down.

"They got their amp working, which was a good thing because our backup was behind everything. It would've taken us an hour to get to it."

Their waiter came over and set a tray down at their table, then passed out their meals. "Here's your asiago and spinach-stuffed chicken," he said as he set a plate in front of Elise. "And a grilled New York strip steak for the gentleman, salmon with Boursin dill cream sauce for you, sir, and a stuffed Portobello mushroom cap for the lady."

They all said thank you, and as soon as the waiter turned to grab his tray and stand, Elise must've thought the coast was clear enough because she flashed him a smile that definitely said more than "business acquaintance." He returned the smile, knowing full well that his said a lot more, too, then started cutting into his steak.

"You've been here two and a half weeks now," Graham said. "How are you liking it?"

"About four billion times better than I thought I would." He purposely kept his eyes from traveling in Elise's direction at all. "You know how much this physically pains me to say so, but you were right. When I was so narrowly focused on one thing, I lost the ability to think creatively. Since I've been here and doing everything Elise has had me do, I've had so many ideas I never would've been able to come up with before. I can't wait to share them with you when I get back."

Graham wore a pleased smile. A little bit self-satisfied, too. Merit pointed at him with his fork. "Okay, now see that smug look? *That's* why I never say you were right."

Graham laughed a big, hearty laugh and it brought back the Graham he knew. "Fair enough. Okay then, I'll tell you that I had my trip here planned from the start, and I expected to do one of two things while I was here, depending on how you were doing. I'm glad I don't even have to tell you what the first thing was. Since you're doing so well, though, I'll tell you the second."

Merit's interest was piqued.

"The day you left, do you remember that meeting we had with the chief staff?"

He nodded.

"You had everyone choose a goal for the quarter that would take their department forward by a specific, measurable amount, and then you kept a record of the goals."

"I remember." It was kind of a hard thing to forget; it was the very last thing that happened before Graham told him he had to come here if he wanted him to sell his extra two percent. He had been so excited about the goals they came up with and how they were going to meet them. Excited enough it had felt like it could fuel him for running a marathon.

"I had Carla check in with everyone before I left to get their latest numbers. Now I'm not going to give you any specific numbers, but I will say that we are currently twenty percent of the way through the quarter, and every one of your executives, myself included, is at least thirty-four percent of the way to meeting their goal."

"That's fantastic!" Merit said. "Wow." It was as though someone had blown up a balloon inside his chest, making him feel lighter and shoving off all the worries he hadn't realized he had still been carrying.

"They're doing great, Merit. Even without you there. If you've built the company right and hired and promoted the right people—which we have—then you can take vacations and not worry about everything falling apart. You can have a life outside of work, Merit."

He didn't even care that it went against the rules they had just made, he looked over at Elise, smiling broadly. His company was doing great. It was running fine on its own. Everything was going to be okay.

And then he realized something that he didn't think would ever be true: he could have a relationship and his company wouldn't fall apart.

Fourteen

ELISE

"If I could get everyone's attention, please," Christian said from the microphone and Elise turned in his direction, along with everyone else. "The band is ready to begin, and as is tradition with our Midsummer Ball, our dance students will start us off by showcasing a Viennese Waltz. After this first dance, we'd like to welcome everyone else to the dance floor.

"Keep your eyes out all night, though—the Viennese Waltz isn't the only dance they learned, and you'll get several chances to see performances sprinkled throughout. We hope you all enjoy their show against the backdrop of this incredible sunset!"

Merit stood up and held a hand out to Elise. She smiled and accepted his invitation to dance. He led her onto the dance floor as the music began, and they got into position—his hand high on her back, her hand on his shoulder, their elbows high and her arm resting on his, their other hands clasped and held at shoulder height.

"Let's show them how it's done," Merit said.

The music from the live band seemed to enter right into Elise in a way that the music hadn't in the dance room. The one-two-three, one-two-three beat felt as natural to her as breathing. She breathed the cool ocean air in deeply, smiling at Merit as he led her around the dance floor with the natural turn.

"You're on fire tonight," Elise said as Merit led her around the outside edge of the dance floor with such energy and lightness and enthusiasm. The day had been mentally exhausting, but being out here, in the open air, Merit holding her so close, moving together as one, revived her.

Merit's smile lit up his whole face. "I've got more energy than I know what to do with. Does the Viennese Waltz ever include lifts? Because I could put my hands on your hips and lift you high above me, spinning you around like you see the professionals do."

Elise laughed as they did a change step into a reverse turn. "You want to do a lift, for the first time, in front of a crowd when all eyes are on you?"

"First off," Merit said as he spun them in a fleckerl, then Elise leaned back into her contra check, "all eyes are on *you*."

She chuckled.

"I wasn't kidding. Haven't you noticed? You look incredible, Elise. And I'm not only talking about the way you look in that dress, which is pretty incredible on its own. But your stature, your bearing, the way you stand tall and regal and in charge, yet still open and friendly and unassuming. It captivates people. Everywhere you go tonight, people's heads are turning to take you in."

Elise looked into this man's eyes, warm and happy and sincere. She didn't quite believe the part about everyone else watching, but she had never received a compliment from someone before that was so clearly about her and not at all about them.

"And secondly," Merit said, a wry smile on his face, "are you doubting my muscles? Do you think I wouldn't be able to lift and spin?"

Her hand was currently resting on those lean muscles of his, feeling them shift as they moved around the dance floor, and she very much didn't doubt them.

"Because right now I am pretty sure I could lift a car."

"It's been fun seeing you talk business with Graham. Your face lights up and you're practically bursting with energy. I had no idea you found so much joy in it."

He led them in a change step into a natural turn. "It's more than a means to provide for my mom and brothers. The people at my company are my friends, my family. They're home. When I run the company well, I do it to benefit all of them."

As they continued to dance the waltz around the floor, Elise took the moment of being face-to-face with Merit, where by the very nature of the dance she had to gaze into his eyes, to study him. She had been seeing his company as an obsession of his—something that was harming him and making him only care about success. She had only seen the negative sides of it.

But now, after watching him talk about it at dinner with Graham, and seeing how his whole countenance lit up when he heard how everyone was doing, made her realize that there was so much more to it than that.

Yes, he had been holding on to the company so tightly that it wasn't healthy for him or the company, and it had been good for him to come to The Royal Palm to get over that and to gain perspective.

But who he was as the CEO of ZentCube also meant that he was dedicated, passionate, caring, decisive, and in possession of a firm resolve to help everyone he loved. She could now see that there was a lot of good in him being so devoted to his company, as long as he found balance. It made her more determined than ever to help him to find that balance.

As the music came to a close, Merit led her in a fleckerl, but instead of her leaning her head and shoulders back in a contra check, he lowered her into a full dip. As she leaned back, her shoulders resting against his strong arms, she looked up at his face. That caring expression, those kind eyes —she wanted to stretch up and kiss those beautiful lips of his.

But then he pulled her upright. Their faces were inches apart for a small moment, and the music switched to a fast-paced song, perfect for the cha-cha. As graceful as the Viennese Waltz was, it was still a high-energy dance and she was feeling its effects. But she had enjoyed the closeness to

Merit so much that she couldn't pass up doing the cha-cha with him.

They held hands and did the side, rock step, side together side steps that Christian had taught them as other couples joined them on the dance floor, Graham and Tessa included. Merit seemed to want to show off their newfound skills, so it wasn't long before they were separating from side to side, doing spins, and the fall into his arms that they had practiced so much just two days ago.

The more they danced, the less exhausted she felt, which shouldn't have been the case. They stopped for quick sips of water between dances but kept going out on the dance floor when each new song played. They even tried their move where one flung their legs up and around in an arc before the other did, to lots of cheers from the couples sitting at tables as well as other couples dancing.

With each song, she just kept feeling closer and more connected to Merit. As their bodies moved as one through each set of dance steps, she felt as though their minds and emotions were moving just as closely.

They had stopped back at their table to grab another drink between songs when the band started playing a slow song. A perfect song for holding each other close, swaying to the music, her head against his shoulder.

"Would you like to dance, my dear?" Merit said, holding a hand out to Elise.

But Elise's attention was pulled from the dance floor to the beach, where three Midsummer bonfires were burning in a row closer to the ocean, the ocean waves lapping up against the shore just beyond them, the flames casting a golden glow on the water and the sand. She reached out and took Merit's hand and said, "How about a walk along the beach instead?"

He smiled and tipped his head. When they reached the end of the platform, she took off her heels and carried them, the heel straps dangling from her fingers.

As soon as she stepped onto the sand, though, it hit her that, although they got away with touching and hand-holding all night because they were dance partners, they couldn't exactly walk along the beach hand-in-hand without her employees and all the rest of the staff within sight guessing what was going on between the two of them.

And it needed to stop happening between the two of them, so she immediately dropped his hand. Merit threw her a quick look of surprise before remembering, and then he widened the distance between them a bit more. Her hand suddenly felt empty and longing at the loss of his, so she wrapped her arms around herself. How was she going to keep her distance from this man for the next week and a half?

"Are you cold?" Merit asked, moving to take off his jacket.

She shook her head. "It feels good after all that dancing."

They walked down closer to the water's edge, the still-warm sand soft under her feet, getting cooler as she stepped on sand that had recently been touched by the tides. They stopped in front of one of the bonfires, admiring the beauty of the flames with several other couples who had wandered down from the dance floor.

The crackling of the fire was loud, though, the people were too near, and she wanted to be able to talk with Merit as she was soaking in the beauty of this night. She wished she could reach out and hold his hand, pulling him to another part of the beach, missing the closeness they'd been experiencing all night with the dancing. But instead, she just tilted her head in the direction she wanted to go and started walking.

He walked alongside her as they went further down the beach, away from the bonfires and the music and the people.

Merit looked at her curiously. "What are you thinking about?"

Elise thought for a moment, trying to form the jumble of emotions and feelings and images into thoughts. She glanced back to where the Midsummer Ball and the bonfires were growing distant and turned them to walk toward the property and away from the ocean.

"You said the *people* at ZentCube are home. I hadn't ever thought about it that way before. I always kind of thought of home as my house, and hadn't considered how much of that was simply because that was where my mom was and she was 'home.' Since I lived in the same house my entire childhood and then lost the house and my mom so close to the same time, I've never experienced the two separate."

They turned and walked along the sand in front of the row of palm trees that separated the resort grounds from the beach.

Maybe home—the thing that she had been craving so much—wasn't just about her house. Maybe it was about who she shared her life with. She hadn't shared her life with anyone since her mom died. Maybe that's what she had been craving all along. Maybe that's what the longing was that burned in her chest right now.

Maybe she could find *home* with Merit. She reached out and wrapped her hand in his.

Merit looked down at their hands and then met her eyes. "You're not worried about anyone seeing?"

They were getting closer to the Midsummer Ball and all its guests, but they were still a good fifty yards from the nearest bonfire and the edge of the platform holding the tables and dance floor.

"They're all busy dancing, watching the people dance, or blinded by the bonfires." And she needed to feel that same closeness to Merit again. To know if he was "home." She led him through the sand to where three palm trees grew in a clump.

Merit leaned against one of the trees and Elise leaned against the one next to it, facing him.

"So," Merit said, reaching out to brush his knuckles from Elise's temples, down her neck, across her mostly bare shoulders, and down her arm, to where he entwined his fingers in hers. "Did you bring me out here to sneak in a forbidden kiss?"

She dropped her high heels to the sand, stepped closer, and put a hand on his chest, feeling his racing heartbeat beneath his dress shirt. Being out here with Merit felt reckless and daring. "You know what they say: 'Fortune favors the bold.'"

He shifted the shoulder against the tree and reached his free hand up to tuck a lock of hair back into place that had fallen during their dancing. "You're incredible, Elise. Do you know that? More so than anyone I've ever met."

Elise felt the heat of the blush across her cheeks. "And you, Merit, are rather impressive yourself." She ran her hand up his chest until her fingertips just touched the back of his neck. A rush of emotions she hadn't experienced before washed over her as she looked into his eyes, soaking in the kindness, caring, warmth, affection, and the bond of understanding that they had forged.

She glanced at his lips, her heart racing. As he tipped his head toward her, she let go of his hand and wrapped both of hers behind his neck, pulling him to her. Her lips crushed into his, desperate to know if he was what she had been longing for all this time, since long before she even knew he existed.

He met her fierceness at first, his lips pressed firmly against hers, then his kisses slowed. Slow, gentle, caressing. As his lips moved against hers, pressing and tugging, warm and soft, his hands against her lower back, she ran her hands along his strong shoulders.

A warmth fell over her like summer sun on the beach, and she knew she had found what she had been looking for. This man who was so much more than what he had originally seemed had worked his way into her heart.

A *zippp!* sounded in the distance, followed by a boom

that she felt deep in her chest, and light exploded all around her.

Merit smiled against her lips. "You know it's an amazing kiss when there are literal fireworks."

She chuckled. "You know it's a phenomenal kiss when you're the one who lined up the fireworks and it made you forget that they were even happening." Never had a kiss with a fling felt like this. She let out a contented sigh and laid her head against his chest as he turned so they could both watch the fireworks.

Fifteen

MERIT

MERIT USED his keycard to open the front door of his mansion after his run at sunrise, still feeling amazing, even though he'd run six miles instead of four. After his kiss with Elise last night, not only did he feel like he could lift a car, but he felt like he could probably run a marathon to get to the car first.

He was about to head down to the exercise room, but Graham shuffled into the hallway from the kitchen, still in a bathrobe, holding a cup of coffee. "I thought I heard you come in. And I see you're a bit more acclimated to the time difference than I am."

"I can't stay inside sleeping when a beautiful morning like this one is happening."

Graham leaned his shoulder against the wall and just smiled at Merit, and Merit could tell that there was so much more to the smile than he could interpret. Maybe it was that he saw the change in him. A change that, nineteen days ago when Graham first told him he wanted him to take this trip, Merit never would've believed could've taken place. He felt better and more balanced than he had in years.

Or maybe the smile was because Graham had guessed how fully he had fallen for Elise. How much better of a person he was with her in his life. How much he enjoyed being around her. How amazing and beautiful and wonderful and charming and smart and capable she was.

Or maybe the smile was something else. "What?"

Graham smiled down at his coffee and pushed himself off the wall. "You know," he said, looking back at Merit, "I knew you had fallen for Elise when I saw your nerves when you were getting ready for the ball last night. Now I'll admit, I was a little skeptical that Elise felt the same during the first part of the dinner, but I was completely sold by about thirty seconds into your Viennese Waltz."

This time it was Merit who looked down, smiling. Having Elise in his arms all night long, the two of them moving as one, more gracefully than he ever thought he'd be capable of, was the most wonderful thing he had experienced in his life. Even better than ZentCube making the cover of Business Success magazine.

Graham shook his head, chuckling. "By the time two hours later hit and you two were still dancing the night away, moving in unison, looking at each other the way that you were, I think you had convinced everyone in a five-mile radius of that dance floor."

Merit looked at him in alarm. Were they that obvious to onlookers? Would the staff at The Royal Palm buy that they were just performing and that nothing was going on between them?

"So really," Graham said, "the kiss was kind of overkill. I believed you two long before that."

"You saw us kiss?"

"We were sitting on a bench on the other side of the palm trees, taking a break from dancing and enjoying the night. You didn't see us there? I thought that was why you chose to kiss where you did."

Heat rose to Merit's face and he laughed out loud. "No, nope. No. Not our intention. We weren't looking to put on a show."

"For what it's worth, we did avert our eyes to give you some privacy. But I will say that I glanced back a bit too soon, and it looked like it was a pretty great kiss."

Merit smiled. "It really, really was."

When Merit met Elise at the fountain in the center court at ten minutes to ten, she was dressed a bit differently from last night—this time she was in shorts, a t-shirt, and canvas shoes, but she looked every bit as radiant as last night when she'd been in a gown and heels. His smile at seeing her was at least as big as hers was, and he wished he could greet her by cradling her face in his hands and giving her a long, welcome kiss.

But, as it was, he couldn't even reach out and hold her hand. After the hours spent last night dancing, their hands, arms, shoulders, or back touching nearly constantly, he ached to be closer to her.

"So," he said, trying to remember how close acquaintances stood to each other when talking and fairly certain he'd gone over that line, "what's on the docket for today?"

Elise smiled at him in a way that told him that she was aching to step closer to him, too. "Shuffleboard."

"Shuffleboard?" His eyebrows drew together. "That game old people play?"

"It's not just for retired folks," she said, and he walked next to her as she turned to lead him through the grounds to the courts. "But there's nothing like hanging out with people at the sunset of their lives to get a good sense of what is truly important in life. They've got perspective."

They turned onto a shrub-lined path without any other guests around, and Merit said, "You did an amazing job putting together that event last night. Everyone seemed to have a great time. You and your staff should be very proud of yourselves."

Elise looked at him and gave him the most genuine smile he thought he'd ever seen. "Thank you."

Then, in a lower voice, he added, "I, especially, had an amazing time."

She gave him a look back that made him melt a little. He would be heading back to Denver before long. What was he thinking, letting himself fall for Elise this much? They rounded a corner to the shuffleboard courts, where six people, all of retirement age, were already there and picking up the sticks used for the game.

As they neared, Elise said, "Merit, I would like to introduce you to Hank and Mabel Baxter—they're about as much of a staple here as blue skies and sunshine."

The couple had to be in their eighties but still looked pretty spry. "Nice to meet you," Merit said and shook their hands.

"And then this is Roy and Gloria Smith, and those two are Dale and Larry." Merit shook all of their hands.

Mabel held her stick, the end resting on the ground, a sparkle in her eye. "Are you sure you're up for this game? The rating on it is M for Mature."

Larry came closer. "I left my glasses back in my rooms, but I wouldn't say he's got nearly enough wrinkles to qualify as 'mature.'"

"You know, the day I met him," Elise said, winking at him, "I was pretty sure he had a very curmudgeonly soul."

"Then you'll fit right in," Dale said, clapping him on the back.

"The game's simple," Elise said. "You stand here, and as your partner, I'll stand opposite you on the other side of the court. Mabel here is your opponent so she'll be next to you, and her partner, Hank, will be next to me."

"I call black," Hank and Mabel said, nearly simultaneously.

Elise chuckled. "The person with the yellow discs goes first. They just want more chances to knock you out of the point zone. We each have four discs, and you alternate who gets to slide them with their cue. You can't step over this line when you shoot, and your disc has to start in this box. You give it a good push with your cue stick like this." She pushed it with her stick, and the disc slid across the court toward the other end. "It has to go past the deadline—that's the line at halfway—and it can't go past the ten off line at the far end. You want it to land in the ten, eight, or seven-point sections, and you *don't* want it to land in the ten-off section."

"If your opponent's disc lands on a ten, eight, or seven," Larry piped in, "you feel free to knock it with your disc into the ten-off section, though, sonny."

Mabel shook her stick at Larry. "Now, don't you go giving him good advice!"

"That's right," Hank said. "Because Mabel and I are going to win."

"Tell them why," Gloria said.

"Because I'm a very competitive person and I cheat a lot."

Merit laughed loudly. "I'll be keeping my eye on you, Hank."

They started playing, Elise and Hank going first so Merit could get a chance to watch as their discs slid to his end of the court before it was his turn. After all their discs were scored, he and Mabel lined them up on their side.

"I think I'll let the lady win this time," Larry said from his court. Merit was pretty sure it was his version of smack talk.

"It's nice to see that chivalry isn't dead." Gloria gave him a mock curtsy from beside him on their court. Then she lowered her cue and gave him a fierce look that told Merit she was going to give him a run for his money.

It took a few tries to figure out how hard to push with the cue to get the disc to go past the deadline but not to reach the ten-off area. He only landed one disc in a point zone, and Mabel quickly knocked it out with hers at her next shot.

"Take that," Mabel said, doing a little dance.

As players on both courts competed, to much laughter and bantering, Merit found his mind wandering far away from the court. For the last week before the ball, he had found it much easier to stop worrying about his company, and he had gotten more and more used to not having information.

Even though it had felt amazing last night to hear news of his company and to finally get some numbers, in a way, it made everything suddenly much more difficult. It was like when he skipped lunch because he had too much to do. Somewhere in the afternoon, his stomach would get past its initial hunger, and for a while, he'd forget that he hadn't eaten. But then if he had one bite of food, he was suddenly ravenous. The morsel of bread that Graham had brought him was making him hungry for more. It was making all his worries sneak their way back in.

Elise must have sensed that Merit's mind had been wandering to thoughts of his company and how it was doing, because she said, "Now that you've all lived enough life to become so much wiser, what advice would you give?"

Maybe his advice to himself should be to just never take his eyes off Elise, because whenever he looked at her, all thoughts of his company fell from his mind. She was just standing there, cue stick in hand, one end on the ground and the other above her head, looking like a dream.

"I would say," Gloria said, grinning at the shot she just made, "not to give yourself such a hard time. Give yourself a good pat on the back when you just dominated."

"That's right," Roy said from the other side of the court, pointing his stick in emphasis toward his wife. "I'll give you a pat on the back for that one, too!"

"And I would say," Larry said slowly, focusing on lining up his next shot perfectly, "to be patient because better things are coming." Then he gave his disc a good shove and it slid across the court, knocking the disc that Gloria had just shot and pushing it out of the point zone. "Boom!"

As Larry and Gloria tallied up their points, Dale said, "I always figured I'd die young, probably in a fiery car crash. If I'd known I'd live this long, I'd have taken better care of this beauty when I was younger." He motioned to his entire body.

"Hear, hear," Larry said.

Roy lined up his discs in his starting zone. "I'm sure you've noticed, but I obviously heeded that advice in my youth." He held his arm up, flexed, fist clenched like he was trying to show off his muscles, but his short-sleeved button-down shirt was covering it completely. The paunch he had stretching the lower buttons of his shirt didn't help him to sell it, and everyone laughed.

"We have one lifetime to spend here on this earth," Hank said, pointing his cue at Merit. "Don't mess it up.

Don't you wake up at sixty and realize you haven't done all the things you've spent your life dreaming about."

Merit glanced at Elise, and she smiled without looking straight at Merit. He was pretty sure that was one of the main pieces of advice that she hoped they would give. He hadn't agreed with the advice when he had first come to The Royal Palm, but he was getting it now.

He shot his next disc—his fourth one—and it was the fourth one to land in a point area. This was his highest-scoring round yet, and he hoped it would help to pull him out of his deficit.

Mabel lined up her last shot, her focus going from her disc to across the court at his. "And my advice is not to sweat the small stuff. Spend less time worrying." She gave her disc a good push with the cue and it slid across the court, knocking his discs on both the ten-point section and the eight-point section out of the scoring area.

The elderly woman jumped up and down, shouting "Ha ha! Ha ha!" Then she turned to him. "Things always work out in the end. So spending all that time worrying in the middle is pointless."

"Point taken," Merit said.

As Merit and Mabel walked to the other end of the court to score their round, Hank said, "And my advice is to *show* the people that you love that you love them—your mom, your dad, your siblings, your friends, your sweetie. Life gets hectic, but don't forget to say, 'I love you.' Don't just assume they remember." He walked up to his wife and gave her a big smack on the cheek. "Don't let being in public stop you."

Merit laughed a loud, appreciative laugh. Both at the look on Mabel's face and at the irony of Hank's words. If he could, he would walk right up to Elise and give her a big smack on the cheek, too.

"You," Hank said, pointing at Merit, "you make sure that our girl here knows that you love her."

"Oh, we—" He started. "We're not—"

"No," Elise said. "We—We aren't dating. We're just—I work here. And he doesn't. I'm just his personal activities director, and no, Dale, not that kind. I just—"

Elise was floundering, so he stepped in to try to help. "We're just friends. That's all." What was he doing? Elise's job was on the line. He shouldn't be making things more difficult for her.

Roy snort-laughed.

"You two are so adorable," Gloria said. "Now don't you worry. We're all old enough that we've fine-tuned the ability to keep a secret."

"Yep," Mabel said. "We can shut our traps and toss the key with the best of them."

"Well, Mrs. Hamilton can't," Larry said.

Gloria nodded. "True. Stay away from Mrs. Hamilton. But the rest of us—we've got your back, dears."

"Thanks," Elise said and gave Merit a look that said she wasn't sure they were going to be able to pull off the "forbidden" part of their relationship so well.

So he gave her a look back that he hoped said, "Challenge accepted."

Sixteen

ELISE

THE FIRST THOUGHTS that Elise was conscious of making when she woke up were about Merit. She snuggled down into her covers, trying to remember if she'd been dreaming about him, too. Probably so. He had been taking over more and more of her thoughts every day. And the best part of it was, she got to see him all the time. She got to go on an adventure with him every single day. In one of the most beautiful places around.

And she got paid to do it for her job. She really was living the dream.

After putting in so many hours all week to cover for her and to prepare for the Midsummer Ball, Elise told her staff that they could take off anytime they'd like after ten p.m. the night of the ball. A different crew was cleaning up the event and she knew her team needed the break. HallieMae had opted for a getaway and wouldn't be back until tonight, so

159

she wouldn't even have to shower after her roommate had taken all the hot water.

She sat up in bed, hearing the seagulls down by the beach, looking at her bulletin board in the faint pre-dawn light. If all that wasn't great enough, she would also have a home again soon.

Throwing off the covers, she swung her legs out of bed and froze. The picture she always had on her nightstand of her mom and her, grinning from ear to ear as they finished another bucket list item, stared up at her accusingly. She picked up the picture and touched her mom's face. She had made a promise to her a little over eight years ago, and she had managed to keep that promise, unwaveringly, for all that time. Her mom had too much of her respect for her to go back on it.

And now, without her even realizing it, she worried she was very much on her way to breaking that promise if she hadn't already. What was she doing?

She hadn't told her mom she wouldn't date, and she had dated plenty over the past eight years, yet none of them were serious relationships. Several of them even lasted for longer than she'd known Merit. She told herself that made the relationship she had with Merit okay. It meant she wasn't breaking the promise to her mom.

She got out of bed and headed to the shower, not believing the story she was telling herself. Everything with Merit was different, stronger, and deeper than anything she had experienced with anyone else she had dated before. If she was telling herself the truth, this had become a "serious" relationship somewhere around the third or fourth dance lesson, even if neither of them had admitted or even realized it yet.

At six, she met a yawning Merit at the main building, where she got the keys to one of the resort's vehicles.

"You do realize it's four a.m. Denver time, right?" Merit tried to stifle yet another yawn.

"And doesn't it make you feel superior to know that you're up before most of the rest of the nation?"

"Haha. Touché."

It had seemed like the most brilliant idea ever to take Merit kayaking. It was one of her favorite activities to do when she wasn't working, but she didn't get to do it often, since it wasn't something done at the resort itself. There was something about the mix of nature, physical exercise, and the calm feeling of gliding across the water that always made her feel like everything was right in the world. It grounded her and helped her to see any stressful situation in a new light. It helped her deal with whatever she faced.

She knew it would do the same for Merit. Based on what she knew of his daily schedule before he came to The Royal Palm, she doubted that he spent much time in nature at all, except for the occasional executive retreat. The beach was one thing, and actually one of her favorite things out in nature, but there weren't beaches in Denver.

No matter how much time they spent on the sand and

in the water, she worried that once he got back home where experiencing nature in that way wasn't possible, he would eventually forget the difference in how it made him feel.

There were places to kayak in Denver, though. If she helped him to see the beauty of it, then when he was drawn to it in Denver, he could go instead of just shoving the feeling away.

Part of her brilliant idea to go kayaking was also the desire to be with Merit without having to hide the feelings she had for him from every living person at The Royal Palm. Now, though, as she drove them the thirty minutes to the Waccamaw National Wildlife Refuge and Merit reached across the space between them in the Jeep and put his hand on her leg, that idea wasn't seeming like the best way to keep her promise to her mom or the resort. Especially when she thrilled so much at his touch.

Especially because she wanted to lay her hand on top of his and give it a squeeze.

And especially because at every stop sign or light, she wanted to reach out and lay her palm on his cheek or place her hand on his forearm.

After they got checked in at the rental and tours building and put on their life jackets, one of the guides led them down to the wooden dock, where a two-person kayak was waiting for them.

"You've been here before, right?" the twenty-something-year-old employee with a tanned face and long braids asked them. "I think I remember you from last season."

"I have. Merit's new."

"Well, you're in for a treat," she said. "This is one of the most peaceful places on earth. This is a good place to kayak for the first time, too, because the currents are easy, and there are plenty of places to explore." She handed a map to Elise. "Enjoy!"

Elise had Merit get in the front seat so he would have an unobstructed view of the swamps, and not at all so she would have an unobstructed view of him. She climbed into the seat behind him, then using the end of one side of her oar, she pushed away from the dock until there was enough room for her to put it in the water. Then they started paddling down the Waccamaw River.

"For not having kayaked before, you're sure picking up on rowing and steering quickly."

"I had a friend whose dad took us canoeing once when I was fifteen. The oars weren't double-sided, of course, but really, steering is all about logic."

"True."

For a few moments, as they paddled down the slow-moving river lined with cypress trees draped in Spanish moss, she just admired the beauty of his back and shoulder muscles as he worked his oar. That, and the way his dark hair was getting just long enough to bend into little curls by his neck that was now much more tanned than it was when he arrived. Just two days ago, her fingers had been caressing those little curls and brushing along his neck, and she longed to hold him close like that again.

She forced herself to look out at the trees. She had to stop this. She was the kind of person who set goals and relentlessly pursued them. That was who she was. She didn't give in to things that took her away from her goals, no matter how tempting they were. And she was an exemplary employee— it was what had gotten her the job of Activities Director at such a young age. She didn't disobey the rules. That wasn't her.

The river opened into a much wider part, the current slowing. Dry grasses grew in big clusters, coming up right in the middle of the river, the early morning sun shining golden across its surface. They maneuvered through the grasses, and when the river turned down its meandering path and took off in multiple locations, she pointed to one. "Let's go that way."

Their new pathway wasn't much wider than their kayak, the opening between taller, thicker blades of green grasses shooting up through the water. This was her favorite part— where it felt like the river was leaving an opening just for them.

He turned his head to the side. "Guess what I did after shuffleboard yesterday."

"Looked into an AARP membership?"

His shoulders shook from a silent chuckle. "No. I took Hank's advice about showing the people that you love that you love them. I called my mom, every single one of my siblings, and my grandma."

"Really?"

He nodded. "I mean, I call them every couple of weeks anyway—my mom every few days. But usually, it's just to check in to see how they're doing and if they need anything.

I don't usually have time to socialize much except for when we all get together, which isn't often enough. Yesterday, though, Hank's words hit me. I should've been calling at least one of them every day since I arrived."

"That's fantastic!"

"It really was. I was on the phone for more than four hours yesterday."

As she listened to him talk about each of his brothers and his mom and grandma, a deep admiration for this man washed over her, making her wonder how she could've ever not known that he had a heart of gold from the beginning.

The more he talked of his family, a longing for home hit her harder than it had for a very long time. Her mom had a sister, Elise's aunt Karen, who she talked to every once in a while. Maybe she should take Hank's advice and call her more often, too.

But she longed for more than that. She wanted the closeness of family. Her life was full and beautiful and amazing, and she had vowed to herself long ago that she would enjoy fully whatever life brought, and that she would take in and be present for every minute of it.

Sometimes it kept her from realizing exactly how strong that craving for family was. She wiped a tear from her eye, grateful that Merit was the one in front so he couldn't see that she was having a mini-crisis.

Her entire family had just been her mom. That was the person she had made promises to—one on her deathbed saying that she would live life fully, and one at sixteen saying she wouldn't go off and make choices that would mean starting her own family before she was twenty-five. She didn't intend to break either promise.

She just needed to buy her house. That was all. It would fill the void.

Besides, Merit was leaving in just over a week. She was staying at the resort for at least another two months, but more than likely it would be a few months longer than that. She wanted to spend the winters in Nestled Hollow, which was only about an hour and a half's drive to where Merit would be going back to.

She wanted to keep her job as director here, though, and that would take a lot of planning to be able to go home for the winters if Cyree even approved it. And by then, who knew how Merit would feel about her? Letting her heart get so wrapped up in him wasn't wise at all. She just needed to keep her heart safe. She couldn't distance herself from him physically, since she was still his activities director, but she could emotionally. She was used to making hard goals. She could do this.

Then Merit noticed that the land to the side of them wasn't the edge of a river; it was a small island. And with childlike wonder, he asked if they could stop and explore it. She was an exemplary employee and this was exactly the kind of thing that would help Merit, so of course she led him to the best place to go ashore. And to the trail that led to the coolest places to explore. She pointed out some deer, beaver homes, bird nests, and all the different types of birds they ran across. And because the ground was so uneven, they had to hold hands as they walked.

And, because it held the most beautiful view of the vast freshwater wetlands, she led him to the highest rise on the little island, where the trees shielded their eyes from direct sunlight, yet still let them see the morning sunlight shining like glitter across the water.

Which also happened to be the perfect spot to kiss.

He took a step closer to her, then reached a hand out and brushed the hair off her cheek. Then both hands were on her face and he leaned in and his lips met hers. She wrapped her arms around his waist, pulling him closer, and kissed him back.

She let out a happy sigh as he leaned his forehead against hers and said, "I've been wanting to kiss you so badly since the ball. Well, okay, since before the ball."

She chuckled. "So that's the real reason you wanted to explore this island, isn't it?"

He laughed and turned to face the view, his arm around her waist, then winked. "I just knew that you'd bring me to a view that could rival fireworks."

She looked out at the view. "You only have eight days left here. How do you feel about your stay so far?"

"I feel incredible. I'm a little afraid of heading back to real life."

"Afraid? How?"

"I understand what Graham was trying to get me to learn when he sent me here. I thought it was ridiculous at first, but now I get it. I'm just worried that when I get back, regular life will get busy and I'll forget and fall back into my old ways when I no longer have you to guide me."

Why did she want him to ask her to come back with him so badly? It wasn't like she was willing to leave the resort. Working at The Royal Palm also helped her to fulfill the promise that she'd made to herself— that she would spend her life helping others to fully live theirs.

"Well, we've got eight days." She reminded herself that she needed to distance herself from him emotionally. "We'll just spend them getting you good enough at it that you won't need a guide."

Merit looked like he desperately wanted to say something, but held back. Instead, he looked out across the beautiful wetlands and stayed quiet.

MERIT HAD SPENT a glorious morning learning to surf. He knew enough to know that surfing would be hard and thought he'd be embarrassed at all the failed attempts it would take. Or at least he would've thought that before getting to know Elise. She'd had him do plenty of things that he'd never tried before, and she had never made him feel incompetent for messing up. She always gave off the vibe that she thought of him as a hero every time he was willing to try something new.

It hadn't mattered that the morning with Elise was spent in public and that they had to hide their attraction. Just being around her was enough. As they sat on their surfboards, legs dangling in the water, waiting for the next wave to come, she told him stories of her time at the University of Denver and it only made him want to know more. To know everything about her.

As he sat in the golf cart, though, being driven back to his mansion, fears about his company started trickling into his mind. It was great that the company had done so well for the first couple of weeks that he had been gone, but it was feeling like he had been ignoring it for too long. Like he had crossed from a "healthy amount of time away" into a "danger zone."

He wondered if he could talk Graham into giving him some more numbers. Or to at least have a chat with him about how each department was doing, even if he didn't give numbers. Or have a planning meeting. Anything to help him feel like he was doing something.

His phone buzzed in his bag, and he pulled it out just as the driver stopped in front of his place. He gave the man a distracted thank you and a tip as he grabbed his bag and swiped to answer the call. "Edison."

"Merit. I'm so glad I finally caught you. I've been trying all morning."

"Is it Mom?"

"No. Asher. He's relapsed."

"What? I just talked to him two days ago! He seemed fine."

"You know how good he is at hiding it. I stopped by unannounced and caught him in the middle of a bender purely on accident. It's..." He paused a moment, "Well, it wasn't just a weekend thing. It has gotten pretty bad."

"Bad enough to be admitted into a treatment program?"

"Very much so. Mom's spent the morning finding the best place she can find with an open spot. They're headed there now."

Merit paced back and forth, needing to do something other than just stand there. "Is there anything I can do to help?"

"We won't even be able to visit him for a few weeks at least. So there's not much any of us can do right now. And trust me—I know how much that feeling sucks."

"You found out he was in trouble, though," Merit said. "That counts for a lot."

"So does paying for the best treatment. What you're doing counts for a lot, too."

Merit couldn't trust his voice to come out steady, so he didn't say anything.

"Listen, Merit. There's nothing at all we can do right now, but he's going to be okay. He's got the best help there is —including us. I'll keep you updated every time we get any news."

"Thanks, Edison."

Merit hung up the phone and paced back and forth on the road in front of his mansion, still wearing his swim trunks and covered in sand. People fought their way past this kind of thing all the time. He just needed to wait and pray his brother would be okay. And keep providing him with the best care there was.

And the only way to do that was to make sure that ZentCube kept doing well.

He used his keycard to unlock his door, then went upstairs to his room and paced some more, feeling like he was doing nothing at all to help. If he were home, he would be throwing everything into his business right now, making sure it was strong so Asher could be strong.

But here, he could do nothing. Here, he was off playing in the ocean—he looked down at the time that the first missed call from Edison came in—for three hours, oblivious to the fact that his brother was in danger.

And just like playing in the ocean distracted him from the call, he worried that his relationship with Elise was going to distract him from running his company well. And right now, he needed more than ever to run it well.

Hours later, Merit still worried about his brother and felt awful that he wasn't doing anything to help fix it. The sun was setting, which was the time that he usually went for a walk along the beach, so he headed out, hoping it would help.

But he still felt miserable.

He stopped on a stretch of sand next to some bungalows. Once when they were on the beach, Elise pointed at the group and said that was where she lived. He didn't know which one was hers, but he did know that he needed Elise more than he had before. He pulled out his phone and texted *Can you come out and walk with me on the beach?* then clicked send.

ELISE: Just the two of us? In public?

MERIT: Please. It's important.

ELISE: Yes, of course. I'll be right there.

Moments later, Elise emerged from between two buildings wearing sweatpants and a t-shirt, with her hair pulled up into a ponytail bun. "Hi," she said, smiling. Then the smile fell from her face. "Merit, is everything okay?"

He shook his head. And then he told her everything about Asher—his history with rehab and his current situation. The sun had set, but the moon was big and made it easy to see. So as they walked along the beach, they were in plain sight of anyone who happened to be looking or who was on the beach themselves. Even still, she reached out and held tight to his hand.

"And there's absolutely nothing I can do to help."

She stopped walking and faced him, the slight breeze blowing the strands of hair that hadn't made it into her bun. "I think that's the worst part—how helpless it makes you feel."

He nodded. That's exactly how he felt. Helpless. And worried.

Elise must have sensed it because she wrapped her arms around his midsection and held him tight. He wrapped his arms around her, too. She didn't let go—she just kept hugging tight, and he drank in all the comfort and strength she provided.

Eighteen

ELISE

ELISE LOOKED through the meeting agenda she had on her phone, volleyball under her arm and bag hanging from her shoulder, as she walked onto the sand volleyball court for her eight a.m. Wednesday staff meeting. She stifled a yawn as she set the bag and ball on the nearby picnic table. Merit had needed a friend last night, and she had stayed on the beach with him for hours, letting him talk through worries about his brother and ideas of how to help him.

But right now, she needed to get her head in the game. She knew from the past couple of summers that she and her staff would be exhausted by the time they pulled off the Midsummer Ball and that they'd be behind on everything else once it was over. Now that they'd had a break, it was the time to really step things up and get back on track. Elise bumped the volleyball up in the air over and over as she waited.

HallieMae came from the direction of the staff bungalows and Zabrena and Kale from the parking lot, but all within moments from each other, putting them all there at eight on the dot.

"Good morning!" she said as they all neared the picnic table to set their bags down. She bounced the volleyball on her knee. "How was your break, and how did activities go yesterday?"

Everyone mumbled "Fine" and sat down at the table, looking like she wasn't the only one who was tired today. Even still, this was quiet for them.

"Okay," she said, "good to hear, I guess. What about the Midsummer Ball? Any issues we ran into that we should think about doing differently next year?"

When no one responded, she bumped the volleyball to Kale, and he set the ball back to her. "You shouldn't have been so nervous about having to dance in front of everyone," he said. "You did great."

"Thanks! It surprised me, too."

She bumped the ball to Zabrena, hoping that a little movement would wake up her staff. But Zabrena just caught the ball and set it down on the table.

"So, that rule about not dating guests," Zabrena said, "that only applies to us? You're exempt?"

Her eyebrows flashed up in surprise. How had she known? *The dancing.* She figured that everyone who saw them dance would just assume that anything that passed between her and Merit was part of the performance, but she hadn't exactly been thinking of her staff specifically. These weren't people she could tell half-truths to.

Which also meant that she couldn't just tell them that she was helping Merit to meet his requirements as part of her job. The sentence alone was the truth, but not even close to the whole truth.

"And don't even try to deny it," Zabrena said. "HallieMae left as soon as the dancing started, but Kale and I saw you and Merit all night. And we saw you both sneak off for a walk on the beach."

"I didn't need to see it," HallieMae said. "Half the staff all around the resort is speculating about you two. And of course, they ask *me* for details, because as your roommate, they assume that you would've told me."

The hurt she caused her friend was all over her face and in her voice. She should've gone to HallieMae about it long ago.

"There's a rumor going around that you two kissed on the beach," Kale said.

Elise squeezed the bridge of her nose with her thumb and forefinger.

"So is it even a rule?" Zabrena asked. "Because I have friends who work in other parts of The Royal Palm, and half of them say that people in their department date guests all the time and don't get into trouble for it. Is it just something you made up so you would get the first crack at any guest you wanted?"

"No." Elise let out a long, slow breath, the scope of the implications of the last several days with Merit finally sinking in. "Cyree and Devin have explicitly said that they don't want staff dating guests, because when breakups happen, it will affect whether or not a guest will come back to stay later. So yes, it's a rule. A rule I never, ever intended to break."

She hung her head, ashamed. "Although technically we haven't gone anywhere that we wouldn't have gone anyway to fulfill my role as his activity director, I have very much fallen for Merit."

Being the kind of employee that people could look up to, the kind of employee that The Royal Palm would be proud of, was very important to Elise. It was one of her highest priorities, yet she had let the resort down and let her staff down. A dark heaviness felt like it was draped over her.

She looked up and met her staff's eyes. "It's a rule that I broke, and as your boss, I know that makes it an even bigger offense. I apologize. You all deserve better than that from me. I will find a way to make this right." She glanced at her phone that held the meeting's agenda. "If you'll excuse me, I'll send out the notes for this week's staff meeting over email, so make sure to check it later."

She paused, taking one more long look at this group of people who she respected so greatly, knowing that she had lost their respect. And even worse, she had lost their trust. She knew that if she could get either back, it wasn't going to be easy. She took a long slow breath. "I *will* make it right."

Then she walked away from her staff, regret and remorse filling the pit of her stomach with a heaviness that weighed her down. She didn't have a clue how, but she was going to find a way to fix things.

Nineteen

MERIT

MERIT WOKE up from a night of frustrating dreams. Dreams where he was trying to push impossibly heavy objects that wouldn't move. Dreams where he was trying to solve unsolvable math equations. Dreams where he was running as hard as he could push himself, but wasn't moving forward at all.

So he got up and put on his running shoes, just so he could prove to himself that it wasn't real. As he ran along the beach, though, actually making forward progress, he started thinking about ways he could push his company forward, and came up with roadblock after roadblock, just like in his dream.

When his mom had first been diagnosed with cancer nearly four years ago, ZentCube was still new. They had fewer than a dozen employees, and half the time they weren't sure they were going to make payroll. He hadn't had the resources to get her the best doctors and the best treatments and the best care. He knew that the mortality rate for her particular cancer was high, and being faced with the very real possibility of his only living parent being killed by cancer made him want to do everything possible to increase her chances.

But he didn't have money. None of them did. His next oldest brother was twenty and his youngest brother had been thirteen.

Not being able to do anything to help his mom scared him. It was what had given him the biggest drive to constantly push ZentCube to become bigger, better, stronger, and more able to surpass the competition. It was what had led him to constantly seek to learn and refine his skills and find ways to attract the best employees. He pushed and pushed and pushed because he never wanted to be in a position again where he didn't have the resources to help his family.

And now his brother needed those resources. He had been in rehab before and hadn't been able to kick his addictions. He needed greater help than anything they had done for him before, and he needed it long-term to get past the obstacles that caused relapses. And that kind of help was expensive. That kind of help required his business to be on top of its game.

As he was walking into his mansion after his run, he felt the buzz of a text from his phone. It was Graham, just checking in, asking him how everything was going. Instead of responding over text, Merit called him.

"Merit! How's it going, buddy?"

"Asher's in a treatment facility. He's not doing well."

"Oh. Man. I am so sorry. That's rough."

"How are things going with Fèvre Cosmetics? Have we closed the deal yet?"

"Merit—"

"Have we?" he asked more forcefully.

"No."

"I have an idea that I think will get them fully on board. I'm going to contact their CEO, but I'm going to need our current data numbers."

"I don't think that's a good idea. That wasn't our deal, Merit."

"Our deal was before Asher. I need to move this company forward, and this is a very big way to do it. You know what closing with Fèvre will do for our company."

Graham paused for a moment, then said, "If I give you those numbers right now, Asher won't be the only one relapsing."

Merit ground his teeth together. His drive to help his company meet the ambitious goals they set was nothing like Asher's drug and alcohol problems, and it wasn't right for Graham not to bend right now. "It's not the same thing and you know it."

"You're right. It's not. But I still care for you, my friend. The progress you've made in the past three weeks has been incredible. I want you to be able to keep that. The company is doing just fine and will continue doing so for the next week until you return. You have everything you need to help your brother right now."

"Graham, the *only* thing I can do to help my brother right now is to help the company. And I need those numbers to do that. I can't sit here and do nothing."

There was a long pause on the other end of the line while Merit held his breath. Then Graham said, "I feel for you. I really do. It's a hard thing to watch your brother go through something like Asher's going through. And I'm sorry, Merit. I think that giving you the numbers is a phenomenally bad idea."

"And I think you're wrong," Merit said.

"I respect that opinion. But I'm still not going to change mine."

Merit let out a frustrated growl then hung up the phone, hurried up the stairs to his room, and turned on his laptop. He opened the bookmark with his email login screen and typed in Graham's email address instead of his. For the password, he started typing in different letter and number combinations of the word Graham had said out of character—*phenomenally*.

It only took four wrong tries. The fifth time, ph3n0m3n@1Ly got him into Graham's email account.

He scanned through the emails, looking for one from the ZentCube servers that gave an update on the numbers. All the executives had access to all the numbers—he just hoped that Graham had set his notification preferences to get them all instead of just the ones for the Technology Department.

As he looked through the list of senders, his eyes fell on

an opened email from Elise Stevens that had as the subject line "Merit."

He glanced over at the date—she had sent the original email on Monday, so two days ago when they had gone kayaking. He hovered the mouse pointer over the email, trying to decide whether to click on it.

Finally, curiosity got the best of him and he clicked.

 Graham,

Today, Merit and I went kayaking through the freshwater swamps at the crack of dawn. I wanted him to be out in nature, and to remember the healing powers that it has. I think he had a pretty great time! I'm hoping that he'll want to search out some of the kayaking locations once he gets back to Colorado. We were too in the moment to get pictures but trust me, it was absolutely beautiful. And there may have been a pretty amazing kiss in the middle of a small island.

Elise

Merit smiled at the memory.

And then, as he was about to close out of the email, his eyes caught on the response below it from Graham and he paused. Then he scrolled down to see it.

Nice work, Elise! You're doing even better than I had hoped back when we had our first conversation. When I offered you that $20,000 bonus, I honestly didn't know if you'd be able to pull it off. But I'm impressed! It looks like you'll be getting that down payment on your childhood home after all.

No. This couldn't be right. The words on the screen swirled and fogged as his mind did the same. He kept staring at it, but all he could see was the $20,000 right in the middle of Graham's email. He shut the laptop and stood, running his hands over his face and through his hair as he paced.

Don't overreact, he told himself. *There could be an explanation.*

He shook out his hands as he walked. *Figure this out, Merit. What's the explanation?* He talked it through out loud.

"Okay, so Graham is Graham. And when he was lining all of this up, of course, he would've offered a bonus to Elise. That is totally a Graham thing to do. He probably offered one to Elise's boss, too. It probably took a few 'bonuses' to get this mansion on short notice. And tickets to the Luau and the Midsummer Ball. And of course, Elise accepted Graham's offer—she hadn't even met me at that point, and she really wants that house."

The truth was, he was happy for her. He knew how hard she was working and saving to get it. He liked that he was helping.

He stopped pacing, deep in thought. "I guess the real question becomes," he said out loud, trying to form his jumble of thoughts into one coherent one, "what, specifically, did he ask her to do?"

Did he ask her to stick with Merit to the end, no matter how difficult he was? Did he ask her to help Merit meet all goals Graham had set for him? Or did he ask her to pretend that she liked Merit?

"No, stop," he told himself. One of the things that he loved about Elise was how genuine and nonjudgmental she was. They had too many moments when they had connected emotionally too deeply to be faked. He couldn't believe she was being paid for that.

He was just tired from not sleeping well and mentally exhausted from worry about Asher. He flopped down onto the bed and forced his thoughts to calm.

And then, unbidden, thoughts about the Midsummer Ball crept into his mind. Elise had been so nervous about her staff realizing something was going on between her and Merit when they were with Graham and Tessa. Could it have been because at the same time she was trying to convince the staff that she wasn't dating Merit, she was also trying to convince Graham that she was?

And Graham had mentioned several times that Tessa was a great judge of character. At the dinner, she seemed to question how much Elise wanted to be with Merit. Had she seen something that Merit hadn't?

And then Graham's comment the morning after the ball came back to him. The one where he had thought that they had kissed in front of him on purpose. Elise was the one who had chosen the spot next to the palm trees on the beach where they had kissed. If that $20,000 that Graham had offered had been for her to develop a romantic relationship with him, did she lead him to that spot to kiss so that Graham could have proof that she was doing her job?

With each thought, another dagger went into his heart. Could it all have been fake?

No. He wasn't buying it. He needed to talk to her and find out the truth before he would believe that.

ELISE

ELISE DIDN'T EVEN KNOW what to do to make this big of a mistake right. How did she let herself get to this point with Merit? She knew the rules! She made sure her staff knew them well, so it was on her mind often. It was stupid to even put herself in the position to get romantically involved with him.

When she had first gotten the idea to date Merit as a way to help him with the five dates Graham asked her to help with she should've squashed it right away. It had felt like such a small thing—something barely taking her off course. But then the further they got down that road, the more they opened up to each other emotionally, and the more they really started seeing each other.

The only way she could even fathom to make this right was to break up with Merit, then confess to Cyree and Devin about what she had done and accept whatever consequences they felt were right, even if that meant losing her job. They were fair bosses, but this was a pretty big mess-up on her part. Then she would need to let Graham know what had happened and she had no idea at all how to make things right with him. Or to her staff. All she knew was that she had some hefty apologizing to do all around.

But the absolute worst part of all of it—the part that she couldn't let herself think of unless she wanted to fall apart—was what her making things right with everyone else would do to Merit. He had come so far in twenty-two days. He had less than a week left at the resort. Maybe HallieMae could take over as his personal activities director, and Elise could cover for HallieMae.

Maybe it would be better to go talk to Cyree and Devin first, so they could approve the switch to HallieMae before she talked to Merit. She was pulling out her phone to text Cyree's assistant to get a meeting set up when a text came in from Merit.

> MERIT: Can we talk? The sooner the better.

Oh no. She hoped he hadn't just gotten more bad news about his brother. After seeing how it affected him last night, she wasn't sure he could take more bad news. How in the world was she going to break up with him right now?

> ELISE: I can meet right now. Are you at your mansion?

> MERIT: Yes.

ELISE: I'll be right there.

Merit met her at the door and led her inside to a place at the resort that she'd never entered before. The expression on his face told her that he'd had an even worse time this morning than he'd had last night. "Is everything okay with Asher?" She reached a hand out to his cheek, but he turned to lead her to a small sitting room just off the high-ceilinged lobby, so she dropped her arm.

Before he reached the room, though, he turned around, like whatever he had to say couldn't wait any longer. "Is Graham offering you an extra twenty thousand dollars for you to date me?"

She closed her eyes. This was bad. Looking back, if she had told him about the bonus at the beginning, it probably wouldn't have been bad. He likely would've been embarrassed, but he would've understood and wouldn't have been offended, she was sure of it.

But the truth was, she hadn't even thought about bringing it up. Merit had known that it was her job to be his activities director—a job that she was getting paid to do. Somehow, her mind had just lumped the regular pay from the resort and the bonus from Graham together, and it hadn't occurred to her to say anything about it.

"Merit, I am so sorry."

And for him to find out about it right now when he was already dealing with so much worry and stress with his brother. And right when she needed to break up with him.

"When Graham offered the bonus, I was just thrilled that I had shouted to the universe that I wanted to buy my childhood home and it answered with a gift in my lap. But now—now it feels like I've betrayed everyone I care about."

She saw the hurt in his eyes. A hurt she wanted to reach out and fix. She wanted to comfort him, to hold him, to take away all the pain. Not just the pain she was causing, but all of it.

She wanted to spend every last moment he had here with him, by his side in everything. She wanted to go back home with him to Colorado and experience every bit of who he was when he wasn't at The Royal Palm.

She wanted to cheer him on as he worked to grow his company.

She wanted to mourn with him when someone in his family was hurting. She wanted to celebrate with him when someone in his family experienced success.

She wanted to continue to learn more and more about this man who she had judged so wrongly at the beginning and find out all the ways in which he was an incredible human that she hadn't even seen yet.

And she so very much wanted to not be ending things with him right now.

"So it's all true? All this with me was just another goal that you were relentlessly pursuing?"

She wanted to wrap her arms around him. She wanted to lay her head on his chest like she did last night and ease those worries and fears on his face, just like she had done when it was Asher who had caused the pained lines instead of her.

"It is. Merit, I've messed up pretty badly, and I'm trying to make it right." So many tears welled up in her eyes that everything was a blur.

She let out a humorless laugh and batted away her tears. "Which is so stupid, because there's no way to make this right. None of this is right. I can't just make the pain I've caused disappear. I am going to contact Graham today and let him know that I'm forfeiting the bonus. I am sorry, Merit." She sniffed and wiped away another tear. "I'm sorry for all of this, and I'm sorry that I can't see you anymore."

She watched as he broke even further, the expression on his face crumbling even more. Somewhere along the way, she had fallen in love with this man, and to know that she was the one who caused that look on his face was forever going to haunt her.

It took a couple of hard swallows before she could trust that her voice would come out as more than a croak. "I'll talk to Cyree and get HallieMae as your personal activities director for the rest of the time that you're here."

"Don't bother," he said. "I'm heading back home to Denver later today."

"You are?"

He nodded and took a step toward her, pausing, searching her face before saying, "Goodbye, Elise." Then he turned and headed up the stairs.

She watched him until he turned down the hallway. It took a few more minutes of staring at the empty hallway before she managed to let herself out of the house and slowly walk to the golf cart. Another cart passed her as she walked, and she looked up to see Hank and Mabel Baxter waving. She waved back, and Hank stopped their cart.

"You okay, dear?" Mabel asked.

"I'm fine," Elise said, waving them off. They hesitated a moment, and then thankfully drove off without trying to talk to her more.

It took a few minutes of sitting in the cart before she could turn the key. A visit to Cyree would have to wait. The only thing she could manage right now before falling apart was driving back to her bungalow and making her way into her room.

That, and sending off a text. She pulled out her phone and typed in a text to the couple who had bought her home from her six years ago. Putting it off was only going to make things more painful, and she knew they needed to sell quickly.

ELISE: Go ahead and list your house for sale. I'm not going to be able to buy it after all.

The response only took a moment to come in.

HOMEOWNERS: Are you sure?

She typed *Yes*, and sent the message. Then she turned the cart around and headed back toward her bungalow.

 Twenty-One

MERIT

THE FLIGHT back to Denver had been fitful and late, and so had his night's sleep. Merit was still on South Carolina time, though, so waking up early happened whether he wanted it or not. After he showered, he sent off a text to Graham as he finished getting ready.

> MERIT: Things didn't work out at The Royal Palm. You can keep your 2%.
>
> I'll be in the office today, so I'll need my access turned back on.

When Graham's text reply came in, it simply said, *I'll let I.T. know.*

Merit got to the office before any of his executives or Carla arrived and went straight to his desk for the first time in twenty-four days. He turned on his computer and logged in, and pulling up the ZentCube data worked. He was back on the company servers once again.

He threw himself into work with as much ferocity as he could, hoping that all the thoughts of Elise would be drowned out by diving back into what had been one hundred percent of his life before he met her.

Still, though, between emails, or as he was switching over to another view of the ZentCube numbers, he would suddenly find himself with his phone in hand, looking at pictures of him and Elise, remembering how it had felt to see her every single day. Remembering the way the hair by her ears would start to curl after they'd been on the beach, even though the rest of it was straight. Or the way her eyes would crinkle at the sides whenever she would laugh, which was dozens of times a day. Or the way she would rub her thumb on his hand when hers was clasping his.

She had offered him so much of herself. Her view. Her way of looking at the world that was so different from what he was used to. Her spontaneity. Her sense of fun. Her nonjudgmental encouragement. Her praise. Her spunk. Her past. Her dreams, her goals, her hopes. He had soaked it all in, letting it change him for the better.

He should've known that it was all too amazing to last. He should've expected it to be just some beautiful moment specific to his time at The Royal Palm. But he'd let himself start to dream of a future together with her.

Graham knocked on the window beside his office door before stepping inside. "How's Asher?"

Merit shrugged. "It's a long, tough road, but from what we've heard, he's doing well."

"And Elise?" Graham asked. "How are you holding up?"

"Fine," he said. "I see we have a meeting with the technology managers at nine."

Graham nodded, seeming to understand that Merit couldn't talk about Elise right now. "We do. I'll send you the agenda."

He turned and left, and Merit closed his eyes and tried to put all memories of Elise and The Royal Palm into their own little room in his mind. He couldn't have them roaming about like they had been for the past twenty-four days if he wanted to still be able to function.

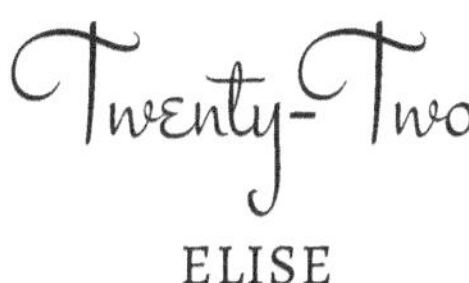

ELISE

ELISE ENDED up not being able to talk to Cyree and Devin at all the day before as she had planned—her emotions had been too on edge to talk to anyone. She couldn't stay closed up in her room and not suffocate, either, yet practically every inch of The Royal Palm was covered in memories of Merit.

Thankfully, HallieMae had been willing to cover for her at work, so she had put on her hiking boots, left the resort, and headed to the Horry County bike and run path and hiked through the switchbacks, twists, and turns of the hilly dirt pathways.

When she got to the river, she found a spot on the bank that was fairly smooth and sat down. As she watched the slow-moving waters pass by, she stared at them, unseeing. She had always been proud of herself for keeping her promise to her mom to not have any serious relationships until she was twenty-five, regardless of how strange everyone around her seemed to think the promise was.

But for the first time, she wondered if a big part of the reason why she had been so good at keeping that promise was that it had been fairly easy. With all pressure off on every date, every relationship, to ask herself if it could turn into something more, she had been able to just date people for fun.

And she had a lot of casual relationships along the way that had been great. But looking back at everyone she had dated over the previous eight years, there wasn't a single one of them that she had wished could turn into a more serious relationship.

Not until Merit. And now she wished it with all her heart.

She wished it could turn into a serious relationship without her feeling like she was betraying her mom by breaking the promise she had made to her. She wished it could turn into a serious relationship without betraying all her coworkers at The Royal Palm and breaking the promise she had made to Cyree and Devin when she took the job.

It hadn't been long, but she already felt Merit's absence. The man she had fallen in love with was now separated from her by seventeen hundred miles, and what felt like insurmountable obstacles were between here and there. She pulled her knees up tight to her and rested her folded arms on them, staring down at the river, and let the tears flow until the sun set.

Today, though, she couldn't hide away from the world and mourn. Today she had to face the consequences of her actions. She went into her office because if she was already feeling awful, she might as well get some computer work done, too.

First, she composed a long email to both Cyree and Devin and told them everything. About the agreement with Graham to help Merit find dates, to dating him herself to help him remember how to date, about how the emotions had turned real and she had found herself falling deeply in love with him, about their kiss—everything.

Then she apologized for the harm it caused The Royal Palm and especially her staff, and she told them she would accept any consequence they felt was right, even if it meant resigning from her position.

Then, she sent an email to Graham and told him many of the same things, except in her email to him, she told him she was forfeiting the bonus he had offered. The look on Merit's face when she had broken up with him was never far from her mind, so she also pleaded with Graham that he would look out for this man she loved, and to make sure he was okay.

Over the next several hours, she did every task in the office that she had been putting off for the last few months. There were several things she could be doing that would take her outdoors and around people, but she wasn't in a state to talk with anyone.

Finally, when the work day was over, she headed home to her bungalow. When she walked into her room, her eyes immediately went to the blank spot on her wall that normally held her bulletin board with the pictures of her childhood home and her progress toward buying it. It had been too much of a reminder of painful things that she had taken it down yesterday.

But now, instead of it reminding her of the home she lost when she saw the blank wall, it reminded her of the man she had lost.

MERIT

MERIT HAD JUST FINISHED a meeting with his sales managers in one of ZentCube's other buildings and headed back to his. Normally, he would take the route back where he'd pass by as many of his employees as possible so he could say hello, but this time he tried to avoid as many as possible. No matter what he did, he couldn't even put a fake smile on his face.

Once he made it back to his office, he went inside and rubbed his hands over his face. How was he going to get through this?

He heard a knock on his doorframe and turned to see Graham standing in the doorway. "Can I come in?"

Merit looked down at his watch. "I've been back in the office for nearly eight hours. I'm impressed it took you this long to come knocking at my door."

"You can thank Tessa for that. She was texting me every half hour to wait, to give you more time."

"But now it's been long enough?"

Graham chuckled and meandered into the room, his hands in his pockets. "She just had a hair appointment, so she missed the most recent time to text. That, and I got an email from Elise."

Merit's attention jerked to Graham. He knew that Elise had been emailing Graham nightly updates, so the two of them probably got to know each other pretty well. And he knew that Elise would likely email Graham to tell him that she and Merit had broken up. Still, he felt a pang of longing in his chest at the mention of communication when he hadn't spoken with her in a day and a half. He hadn't gone that long without seeing her in person since they'd met.

"Do you love her?" Graham asked.

"I do. Every night for weeks I've been going to bed more in love with her than the day before. You've met her. You know how incredible she is."

"Yes, and I know that she's brought out the best in you. You're the strong, capable, brilliant Merit I'm used to, but now that's combined with the sense of wonder and curiosity you had when we first met. It's a brilliant combination. When I went to The Royal Palm the night of the ball, I saw in you everything I had hoped I would see. But I also saw the glow of someone who had fallen head-over-heels in love. I really liked that Merit."

He did too. He should've known it wouldn't last.

"So then, why are you here? Why aren't you trying to work things out with her?"

"Because it's not that simple."

He needed some fresh air. He opened the glass door to his balcony and stepped out onto it. It wasn't a large balcony, but it had an incredible view. ZentCube's headquarters was the highest building on a slight incline, and his office was on the side of the building facing all the others.

He leaned his arms on the balcony railing, looking out over every single one of their buildings. They weren't in downtown Denver, where all the buildings were high-rises—this area was one they had chosen specifically because all of the buildings were only one or two stories high, with the exception of the three-story-high headquarters. They loved the feeling of home that it brought.

Graham leaned on the railing next to him, and for a few moments, the two of them just looked across the physical representation of the company they'd built.

"Do you remember four years ago? We were in that crappy building downtown with the toilets that didn't flush right and the wall outlets that only worked half the time."

Merit nodded. "And we were on the floor below that company that liked to do group jumping jacks every hour to get people's blood flowing."

"There were so many times when we questioned whether we should just close our doors and count it all as a failed business attempt. If it weren't for our unfailing belief that we had a great product, I don't think we would've made it."

"Those early days were rough."

"That they were." Graham paused for a few moments. "Until you decided that ZentCube was going to succeed in a big way. Man, you were unstoppable! It was fun to see the fire in your eyes every morning and to see you attack every obstacle so fiercely. Within a week of your mom's diagnosis, I knew that ZentCube would one day be this big, as long as we had you at the helm."

Graham stayed silent for long enough that Merit questioned why he was even bringing this up. It seemed odd after he'd gone to so much work to get him to not put everything he had into the company. Then Graham turned to face him, his side leaning against the railing. "So why aren't you taking that same passion, that fire, and that unyielding determination to win back Elise?

Merit swallowed. "Because I don't think she wants me to."

"What's your proof?"

"My proof? Graham, she broke up with me."

He shook his head. "That's not proof. Give me something else."

"She agreed to a relationship with me to earn the twenty thousand you offered her. It was all fake. I'm pretty sure that's enough proof right there."

"Do you really believe that?"

Merit's eyes flashed to Graham's.

"I offered her the bonus to get you to go on dates—I didn't care who with. I just wanted you to see that dating could be fun again. Elise did the falling in love with you part all on her own. So I'm going to ask you again: do you really believe that your relationship with her was fake?"

Graham waited patiently for him, so he tried to figure

out what he believed. Could it have all been fake? They had spent so many hours together every day, and they had shared so many things with each other that he knew were true. In thinking of all his relationships with all the people he knew—many of whom he'd known for years—Graham was the only one who he could honestly say that he knew on a personal level more than he knew Elise.

And of everything he knew of her, she was nothing if not genuine.

Merit shook his head. "It couldn't have been fake."

"Nope. And I'll tell you how I know that. The two of you decided to do a fake date on the boardwalk, right?"

"You knew about that?"

Graham nodded. "Two days later, she sent me the picture of the two of you playing racquetball. The next night, her kissing your cheek in the Sky Wheel. Then she emailed me the update about the dance lessons. That night, she emailed me a second time to confess that the boardwalk date had been faked and that she felt too guilty to not let me know.

"Then she told me that the others hadn't been faked, but that she wasn't allowed to date you, so the dates needed to stop. She said you weren't going to go on dates without someone pushing you to, and that she could no longer be that someone. She said she was giving up the bonus."

"She did?"

He nodded. "She kept updating me, still, about your progress in general, so on the second week of your dance lessons, I called and told her that if she kept sending me updates, the bonus was back on."

"Why?"

"Because I could tell from both of your updates that the attraction between the two of you was real even if the two of you hadn't figured it out yet. You both fell in love long before either of you realized it."

He met Graham's eyes for a long moment. "Then why did she end things?" And *why* had he not stayed there and tried everything he could think of to work things out?

"She's got her own obstacles stopping her."

Merit turned around and went back into his office—the place where he made big plans. He ran his hands through his hair. "What can I do to fix this?" He wasn't asking Graham for answers so much as he was asking himself. But Graham, two steps behind him, answered anyway.

"I'd maybe start by calling her boss."

Then he headed toward the door to leave Merit's office and to let him brainstorm like he always did when Merit needed to come up with a plan.

"Graham?"

Graham stopped in his doorway, not turning back. "Yeah?"

"You knew from the start that I would fall for her, didn't you? Is that why you chose her?"

Graham turned his head in Merit's direction just barely enough for Merit to see the smile on his face. "Let me know if you need anything."

Then he left Merit alone in his office to figure out what he was going to do.

ELISE

ELISE HEARD the buzz from a notification on her phone and picked it up off her kitchen counter. She froze when she saw the screen. It was a text from the couple who owned her home. She swiped to open the text to read the full thing.

> HOMEOWNERS: We know this isn't the news you wanted to hear, but the house listing went live this morning, and we've been showing it nonstop all day. We've already gotten fourteen serious offers on it. We've accepted one of the offers and let the buyer know. We're sorry. We know how badly you wanted it.

Elise had known this was coming; she just didn't think it would happen so quickly. She let the pain of its loss wash over her and mix with the loss of Merit. She wanted to crawl into bed and take a late afternoon nap and not wake up until all the pain was gone. She was on her way into her room when she got a text from HallieMae.

> HALLIEMAE: I need help! Can you meet me at the beach where we made sand castles?

Oh no. Elise glanced at the time on her phone as she texted back *Be right there.* HallieMae's teen activity should've already ended. Did an accident or something happen with one of the teens? She pushed her phone into her pocket, slipped on her flip-flops, and raced out the door and toward the beach.

When she got close enough to pick HallieMae out of the crowd of people on the beach, she saw that she was just lazily drawing lines in the sand with her big toe as she waited, so Elise slowed her jog to a walk. As she reached HallieMae, she said, "What's wrong?"

"What's wrong," HallieMae said, linking her arm in Elise's, "is that my friend is in crisis. Kick off your shoes and walk in the water with me."

"HallieMae!" she said as they walked to the water's edge, the wet sand sinking slightly with each step. "You scared me! I thought something went horribly wrong."

"It did."

Elise rolled her eyes. "Then why didn't you just come to the apartment and talk to me about it?"

"Ew, no. You've got sadness coming off you in waves. In the apartment it's got nowhere to go, so it just bounces off the walls and multiplies. At least out here, the wind and air can dissipate it."

Elise rolled her eyes. She would've tried to protest it, but she could feel it herself, so she couldn't disagree.

"So," HallieMae said as she led them toward the bungalows and away from the bulk of the guests at the beach, "let's just start this conversation off by acknowledging that you are in love with Merit. You know it. I know it. Can we agree on that?"

Elise nodded.

"Okay, I'm doing a lot of guessing here, since you haven't confided in me about most of this."

"I'm sorry, HallieMae."

"No, I get it. Mostly. Although I think I'm a pretty cool person to confide in, so you should keep that in mind for the future. But that's a discussion for another time. You're sad, obviously, and Merit checked out of the resort. Don't give me that look. Me, Kale, and Zabrena might've done some investigative work after your whole descent into the land of the brokenhearted. Now we've all seen you two together, and it's safe to say that Merit was also in love with you. True?"

Elise nodded. "I think so. I mean we hadn't said the words, but..." She thought about not only their time together since he'd arrived, but the look on his face when she had broken things off. "Yes."

"So you love him and he loves you. Yet he's on the other side of the country, and you're walking around like you've got a rainstorm pouring down on you. The way I see it, you have two issues: the no-dating rule at the resort and your promise to your mom. Am I still on track?"

"Yeah."

"I can't help you out on the no dating rule—that's between you and Cyree and Devin. But I will tell you that I ran into Cyree about thirty minutes ago and she asked me to remind you to check your email once in a while."

Oh no. She really needed to be better about that. She pulled out her phone and opened her email app. There was a reply from Cyree to the message she'd sent that morning to her and Devin. She opened the message and saw one short sentence.

 Meet me in my office to discuss this at 5:30.

She touched reply and typed *I'll be there*, and pressed send.

Elise pushed the phone back into her pocket. "It looks like I don't have too much longer before I need to head over for the meeting."

HallieMae linked her arm in Elise's again and continued walking. "Then I guess we better get talking. Now I'm not saying that you won't have to do some damage control with us, your amazing team, but at least you have the advantage of knowing that we love you, even when we get really mad at you. And know that we still want you as our boss, and we're willing to fight to keep you."

Elise stopped and met HallieMae's eyes. "Thank you, HallieMae. Truly. That means a lot."

"Well, you've been there for all of us. That means a lot to us, too." She smiled at Elise. "Okay, I've been thinking about your promise to your mom, and I realized something super important."

Elise raised an eyebrow.

"Do you know what? Come over here. Let's sit and talk." HallieMae led her away from the water to a drier area, then sat down right on the sand. Elise sat down, too, and HallieMae shifted so they were facing each other. "You made *two* promises to your mom. You don't talk about the second as much. Maybe because it's not as concrete or measurable, or maybe it's because you feel like you've got it covered, so you don't have to think about it much. I think we should talk about that second promise. The one you made on her deathbed."

"Okay," Elise said. This was an interesting turn in the conversation; she wasn't quite sure where HallieMae was going to go with it. "It was only a week or two before she died, and it became obvious that she was going to pass away and that we weren't going to get to any of the things left on her bucket list. We were talking about the last few—one of them was to come here—and she was just so full of regrets for all the things she hadn't done.

"So then she grabbed my hands and said, 'Elise, I want you to promise me that you will live life to the fullest. That you won't look back on the life you've lived and have regrets. You find what makes you happy and go after it with everything you've got.'" A tear escaped and she wiped it away. "And that's why I work here, doing what I'm doing."

HallieMae looked her in the eyes for an uncomfortably long moment, then, almost in a whisper, she said, "If you let Merit go, will you look back on this part of your life with regrets?"

HallieMae's words hit her with such force she flinched. She imagined herself here, at The Royal Palm next summer, thinking back to this summer. And the thought that she had let Merit go made her feel empty and wrong and full of more regrets than she knew how to bear. Merit was the person she had always wanted in her life, but she hadn't known it until she met him.

The realization of exactly how letting him go, after experiencing having him in her life, would make her feel hit her strong and hard. She knew that for the rest of her days, she'd feel like she let the most important thing slip away. She would feel the pain of that regret exquisitely and always.

"She told you to find what makes you happy and to go after it with everything you've got. Does Merit make you happy?"

Elise nodded. Her emotions had grabbed her so tightly that she could barely speak, but she managed to croak out, "What about the other promise?"

HallieMae shook her head. "The two conflict. If you keep one promise, you'll break the other. So I guess the question you'll have to figure out the answer to is if you could talk to your mom, which promise do you think she would tell you to keep? Which one do you think is more important to her?"

The exact moments she had made both promises were

burned into Elise's memory. The dating one had been on a day when the water heater had gone out just four days after the refrigerator had, and the day after Elise had snuck out her window late at night to go to a movie with her friends. Her mom had been particularly frustrated at being a single parent at that moment. She had told her that she didn't want Elise to make a similar mistake and end up having to live such a hard life herself.

The one where she promised to live her life fully was just a few weeks before high school graduation. That one hadn't been an in-the-moment frustration. That one had been a plea from a dying mom to her daughter. It had held all of her hopes and dreams for Elise—all the things that she wanted her to know but wouldn't get a chance to tell her later on. That request had come as if it was from the very core of her soul, trying to impress it in the very core of Elise's soul.

Without a doubt, if her mom had to choose just one promise for her to keep, it would be the one Elise had promised to her on her deathbed. To live life with no regrets and to go after happiness fiercely.

Elise leaned forward and wrapped her arms around her friend and whispered, "Thank you, HallieMae."

As Elise walked to where Cyree's and Devin's offices were in the main building, she took in all of The Royal Palm. She loved this place so much—she had ever since her mom decided it was where she wanted to experience the ocean for the first time. But she loved Merit even more, and if finding a way to convince Merit that they should still be together meant leaving The Royal Palm, it would be worth it.

When she got to Cyree's office, Devin was already seated inside. She walked to the only other open chair that wasn't Cyree's and sat down, trying to inconspicuously wipe her sweaty palms on her shorts as she did.

As Cyree took her seat, she said, "First of all, we would like to thank you for your email, and for coming clean on everything that was happening between you and Merit Casselman."

Elise nodded.

"As you know," Devin said, "we make it a point to treat our employees and our guests fairly. As a director, I'm sure you can appreciate what kind of position it puts us in when someone breaks one of the rules."

Elise swallowed and tried not to drop her gaze to her lap. "I do, and I apologize. I feel terrible, and I'm willing to accept whatever consequence you feel is fair."

"What's *fair* is a little tricky." Cyree stood and walked over to her window. She looked out for a moment before turning back to Elise. "Did you know that each of your staff sent emails independent of each other, all begging to have you stay?"

"They did?" Being on Elise's side in this was surprising enough, but to have them sending requests to the Chief Operators was something else entirely. "Even Zabrena?"

"Zabrena," Devin said, "came to meet with us in person.

She told us that if we needed to fire someone, to have it be her instead of you."

Elise's breath hitched and warmth spread through her.

Cyree walked to the edge of her desk, standing right next to where Devin sat. "We didn't just get emails from your staff. We also got them from a good dozen of our more elderly guests."

Her eyebrows knit together. How would they have even known? Then she remembered seeing the Baxters when she was leaving Merit's mansion.

"It seems that they guessed what might be happening and feared your job might be in danger," Devin said, "so they let us know that their experience here would be negatively impacted by your departure."

Cyree half sat on the edge of her desk. "Here's the thing. We think you should take some time away from the resort."

What did that mean? Were they forcing her to take a leave of absence? Maybe for the rest of the season? She tried to wait patiently for more information.

Devin leaned forward, resting his elbows on his legs. "Like we said, treating everyone fair is important to us. It wouldn't be fair if we took away the boss that your staff is so loyal to. And it wouldn't be fair to our guests if we took away their favorite activities director."

"And we saw you and Merit together the night of the Midsummer Ball," Cyree said. "We decided that it wouldn't be fair to you as our employee if we didn't encourage you to be with someone who you are so obviously in love with."

Elise looked between the two of them, not sure she was hearing everything correctly.

"So we've decided to give you a second chance. And apparently, we aren't the only ones who feel that way. It seems that a few of our more well-off elderly guests thought you should get a second chance, too." Cyree grabbed a file folder off her desk and handed it to Elise. "So they bought you a plane ticket to Denver. We would like you to go, with our blessing. We'll make sure things are covered for you here."

"For real?" Elise looked between her two bosses, then at the folder in her hands. Then she leaped up and hugged them. "Thank you both so much!"

"Now go on," Devin said. "I'm sure you've got packing and other preparations. Your flight leaves bright and early tomorrow morning."

Elise took one last look at her bosses, gratitude for them overflowing. Then she turned and raced back to her bungalow.

Twenty-Five

MERIT

MERIT SAT in his conference room around the large table next to his assistant, Carla, surrounded by his chief officers, his leg bouncing up and down. Everyone's eyes were on Graham's slide show on the big screen, where he was updating everyone on a new proposal for the technology department. One of Graham's biggest pet peeves was boring slides, so he tended to go overboard in the other direction. They were entertaining, to say the least, but Merit couldn't keep his attention on Graham's presentation and off thoughts of Elise.

Carla reached out and put a firm hand on his knee, stopping his shaking leg. "Sorry," he whispered and tried not to annoy everyone around him with his fidgeting.

He took the key out of his pocket for easily the tenth time this meeting and turned it over and over in his hand. It wasn't the actual key to Elise's childhood home—it was more of a symbol to represent it. He knew that Elise had told

Graham that she was giving up the twenty thousand when they broke up, and he had known from their many conversations that the couple who lived there were anxious to sell.

Out of fear that she would lose something that he knew was so important to her, he had taken a trip to Nestled Hollow yesterday to find her home.

He was relieved that he hadn't waited any longer, because it had gone up for sale that morning, and there was a steady stream of people looking at the house. His first instinct had been to buy the house for Elise, put a big bow on it, and give it to her, just to see how happy it made her. He didn't know if he could convince her to reconsider their breakup or not, but he wanted her to have it either way.

Thankfully, though, before he got a chance to speak with the owners, it dawned on him that if he bought the house for Elise, she would probably feel like it was a gift with strings. That it came with obligations to get back together, and he didn't want her choice to be affected by a house. And if they did get back together, he didn't want to have to wonder for the rest of his life how much of her decision had been because of it.

No. When Merit saw Elise and bared his heart to her, he wanted Elise's decision on whether they should get back together to be one hundred percent because that was what she had wanted, not because of some sense of obligation.

Even though Merit hadn't stayed at the resort for the full four weeks, Graham said that Merit had met all the requirements that he set out for him, so that meant that Elise got her bonus. Graham hadn't told Elise yet, though, and Merit had been worried that her house would sell before she even found out about the bonus.

So he met with the owners, put a fair offer on the home in Elise's name, and talked them into choosing her offer. The owners had wanted to sell it to her so badly that he hardly had to do a thing to convince them.

He looked at his watch again. Carla leaned over and said in a low voice, "The car to take you to the airport won't get here for another hour. *Relax.* You let me be the one watching the clock." She looked down at her notebook. "I've got to go check on a couple of last-minute arrangements. I'll be back in five."

This was a meeting Merit should be paying attention to. Normally Graham's presentations were the ones he made sure to be at more than anything else—and not just because of his entertaining slides. Graham was a master at leading the technology team to make groundbreaking improvements to their product, and it was fun to see.

But as much as this was his favorite meeting, he just really wished that Carla would've been able to find an earlier flight. This one wouldn't put him in Myrtle Beach until eleven p.m., and waiting to see Elise was killing him.

"Now between the update we just rolled out to our customers," Graham said, "and the projects we have in the works, I think it will make our customers feel like they can step away from their offices and spend some time on the beach."

Graham switched to a slide that he must've taken when he'd been at The Royal Palm because Merit recognized the beach. Graham also tended to use a lot of sound in his presentations, too, and this one came with sounds of the waves, the seagulls, and beachgoers, and made Merit miss Elise even more deeply.

He shifted in his seat and looked down at his watch again. Fifty-three minutes and his car would be here. His bags were all packed and waiting in his office so he could grab them and go.

"And then while they're on the beach, having access to their company at their fingertips, then they might be available when a beautiful woman walks up." Graham had used his phone to snap a picture of Merit and Elise the night of the ball, and he had animated the slide so that the picture of them slid onto the beach scene.

Merit chuckled and shook his head as all of his executives said things like "Aww," and "Such a cute couple."

Then their focus seemed to all change to the door simultaneously, so Merit turned to see what had gotten their attention.

Standing in the doorway of his conference room next to Carla, right here in Denver, was Elise.

"Elise," he said, practically leaping out of his chair as she raced toward him. He didn't know where the two of them stood yet, but she was here and that look on her face told him that everything was going to work out, so he wrapped his arms around her as they met. Elise squeezed him tight, like she didn't want to ever let go, and that was very fine with him.

Eventually, she pulled back and took his hands in hers. "I

am sorry, Merit. I was just so afraid. I was afraid of letting my mom down, I was afraid of letting my staff down, and I was afraid of letting The Royal Palm down. I was so busy trying to get back my lost home that I hadn't realized exactly how much I had found home with you. I let fear and loss take over and try to stop the most incredible thing that has ever happened to me. I love you, Merit. That's all that matters, and I see that now. Everything else will work out if I have you."

Merit smiled, happiness and warmth spreading throughout every bit of his body, unlike anything he had experienced before. He reached up and ran the back of his fingers from her temple down to her jaw. "You weren't the only one who let fear stop you. I may have let it make me question *us*, even though I'd already gotten all the confirmations to the questions that I needed."

For a few moments, they looked into each other's eyes, and Merit just drank Elise in, feeling like he had been stranded in the desert and she was water.

"My driver should be here in less than an hour to take me to the airport. I had planned to be at The Royal Palm by eleven tonight to convince you to give us another chance."

"Really?"

He nodded. "I worked everything out with Cyree last night. I was going to come to serenade you outside your bungalow, even though I can't sing. And when you came out, I was going to tell you about how much you changed my life, and how much I love every moment I'm around you. About how I love everything about you—your strength, your personality, your heart, your way of thinking —everything.

"And I was going to keep fighting and keep trying for us to be together until you either decided that we should continue to date, or until you asked me to stop."

He let go of one of her hands, reached into his pocket, and pulled out the key. "And regardless of what your answer was, I was going to give you this."

Elise held out her hands and he placed the key in her palms. She looked up at him, confused.

"No matter what happened with us, I didn't want you to miss out on buying your childhood home. Graham said the bonus is yours, so even though the house was in a bidding war, I talked to the owners and they agreed to turn down the other offers and sell to you."

"Merit," Elise said, awe and wonder in her voice. "I can't believe you did this for me. Thank you."

At the sounds of happy sighs and chorus of "Aww"s that came from the room, Merit glanced at the people around the conference table, remembering they were there. Then his eyes glanced at the wall-sized screen on the wall that now showed a picture of Elise's home on the left, with a big key on the right.

Then Graham clicked and a heart appeared behind the key, with the words "Key to her house" above it and "Key to his heart" below it. He wondered when Elise had contacted Graham to let him know she was coming. Carla seemed to be in on it too, and he suddenly wondered if he actually had a car coming to take him to the airport.

"So will you keep dating me? I'd embarrass myself and they'd never let me live it down, but I am perfectly willing to serenade you in front of my executive staff if that's what it takes."

"Of course, I will," Elise said. Then she set the key on the table and, wrapping her arms behind his neck, she pressed her lips to his.

Merit put his arms around her waist and pulled her close, moving his lips against hers, slowly, savoring every moment of having her back in his arms. He chuckled into the kiss as, from Graham's presentation, Barry White's low smooth voice started singing *My First, My Last, My Everything*. They both turned to see that his slide now showed a romantic candlelight dinner.

Merit shook his head. "Maybe we should go to my office."

Graham shook his head. "No, you should not. We've waited a long time for this, Merit. Besides," he said, a grin spreading across his face as he rushed around the table toward the door, "the cake's here. Right on time!"

One of the staff assistants rolled in a cart with plates, forks, napkins, and a giant cake that spelled out in frosting, "Congrats on reuniting, Merit and Elise!"

Merit turned his attention back to the woman in his arms. "Are you sure you still want in on the craziness here? It's not too late to back out."

Elise smiled that big, genuine smile of hers and said, "I am sure. I wouldn't give it up for anything."

Epilogue

Elise shook the snow off her coat and stomped her boots on the ground before getting into her car. She had just finished running the snow activities for a group of tourists who either didn't ski or didn't get enough of the snowy weather from skiing. Even though it was the beginning of March, there were still several feet of snow on the ground. She had thought it would be hard to adjust to the winters in Nestled Hollow after living at The Royal Palm for three and a half years, but it turned out it was just like riding a bike.

She got into her car and drove down the snow-lined streets toward her childhood home. For the first four months after she and Merit had gotten back together, Elise stayed and worked at The Royal Palm, taking trips to Denver to see Merit whenever she could, him coming to the beach with her whenever he could. And video chatting every single night that they couldn't.

The last four months, though, she lived only an hour-

and-a-half drive from Merit, and it had been heavenly being able to see him so often and meeting his mom and all his brothers.

She was sad that he had to work late today, especially since it was her birthday, but they had plans to celebrate it this weekend. Besides, she had a few friends she'd left behind in Nestled Hollow who still lived here, and she'd made some new ones since she got back. Four of them were going to go out to dinner tonight to celebrate not long after she got home.

When she turned onto her street, she was surprised at how many cars were parked along the sides of the road, next to the piles of snow, making the street more difficult to navigate. Usually, her road wasn't so busy. Over the tops of the snow, she saw some unusual colors on her house, but she couldn't tell what it was.

Until she pulled into her driveway. A giant banner hung across her house that read, "Happy 25th Birthday, Elise!" and streamers and balloons were hung everywhere. A couple of dozen of her friends filled the porch and sidewalks and the end of her driveway, all waving their arms and wearing party hats on top of their winter clothes.

She got out of her car, overwhelmed and surprised, and everyone shouted, "Happy birthday!"

Her friend Macie was the first to reach her, and she gave her a hug. As Elise made her way from the driveway to the sidewalk, she greeted each person as she went, blown away that so many of them had shown up to wish her a happy birthday. Halfway up the sidewalk, everyone on the sidewalk and the porch parted to the side, leaving nothing blocking her view of the man on her porch.

"Merit! I thought you couldn't come tonight!"

He raised an eyebrow. "Nothing at work could ever be as important as being with you on your birthday."

She made it through the crowd and to the porch where she wrapped her arms around him and he spun them around once, then dropped her into a dip, just like they had done during the Viennese Waltz at the Midsummer Ball. Except unlike their dance at The Royal Palm, he kissed her this time, to the whoops and cheers of her friends.

When he pulled her back to standing, he said, "I have wanted to do this for months. But out of respect for your mom, I decided to wait until the day her daughter turned twenty-five."

Cocking her head to the side, Elise wondered exactly what he meant, until he dropped to one knee and she knew.

"Elise Stevens, you have made me happier than I ever thought I could be. Please say you'll marry me, and I'll never stop doing the same for you."

Elise looked down at Merit's face, so full of determination and passion and drive, just like when she had first met him nine months ago, but now it also was filled with happiness and joy. Every day she spent with him in her life had been more wonderful than any day without him ever had, and she wanted nothing more than to spend the rest of her life with him.

"Yes, Merit, yes! Of course, I'll marry you!" She pulled him to his feet and, with a hand on each of his cheeks, brought his face toward hers and kissed him—his lips soft and warm and very much home.

"Now come in out of the cold," Macie said. "This isn't just a birthday party—we've got an engagement party happening inside!"

Elise smiled at her fiancé and, holding his hand, led him into her home.

THE END

Author's Note

I hope you enjoyed reading Elise's and Merit's story as much as I enjoyed writing it!

Want to spend more time at the Royal Palm Resort? Grab your copy of the next book in the series, *A Kiss at Christmas,* and you'll get to see Merit, Elise, Graham, and some other favorites again!

Curious to know more about Elise's home town, Nestled Hollow? There's a whole series of books set there! Find out more at www.megeaston.com.

—Meg

A Kiss at Christmas

She wants the perfect Christmas. He wants it over already. But fate has other plans.

Kelli just wants a little perfection in her life. Have the perfect Christmas. Be the perfect daughter. Get the perfect parking spot. Be the perfect employee. And pull the perfect pranks on the adorable but off-limits Parker Brockbank in Trade Shows, the guy she went on a first date with two-and-a-half years ago. The date that was anything but perfect.

You don't always get what you want, and fate has a sense of humor.

Parker wants to ignore Christmas. He usually enjoys it, but since his fiancee broke off their engagement two months ago, canceling his Christmas plans, he doesn't want anything to do with the holiday. All he wants is to move on and go back to being the Parker that pulls pranks on the charming but off-limits Kelli Ellis from Digital and Print Ads.

Fate has a sense of humor with him, too.

Both Parker and Kelli think they're going to be spending the holidays alone. Until the owner of the company they work for—a man who has a secret knack for matchmaking—invites a dozen employees to celebrate Christmas on the beach. With a competition and a prize Kelli and Parker both want, the only way to win is by joining in on the Christmas fun.

And when it comes to winning against each other, Parker and Kelli are nothing if not competitive. Can they get past their workplace rivalry and take a chance on a second date that might just be imperfectly perfect?

Get the Nestled Hollow series

Coming Home to the Top of Main Street
Second Chance on the Corner of Main Street
Christmas at the End of Main Street
More than Friends in the Middle of Main Street
Love Again at the Heart of Main Street
More than Enemies on the Bridge of Main Street

Listen to the audiobooks on YouTube

Meg Easton is the *USA Today* bestselling author of contemporary romances and romantic comedies with fun, memorable, swoon-worthy characters, and settings you'll want to pack up and move to. She lives at the foot of a mountain with her name on it (or at least one letter of her name) in Utah. She loves gardening, bike riding, baking, swimming before the sun rises, and spending time with her husband and three kids.

She can be found online at www.megeaston.com

Sign up to receive her newsletter and stay up to date with new releases, get exclusive bonus content, and more.

If you liked this book please leave a review. Your review can help other readers find books they might fall in love with.

youtube.com/@megeastonauthor

bookbub.com/authors/meg-easton

instagram.com/megeaston_author

facebook.com/MegEastonBooks

tiktok.com/@megeaston_author